The whole place just seemed so . . . <u>British</u>.

There was no other word for it. It wasn't exotic in the way that she imagined the Far East would be. It wasn't idyllic like a Caribbean island. In fact, it was just as dank and gray as she'd been promised. And yet, expansive, color-less, and understated as London seemed, it was, to Abby, completely alive. She was living her *Let's Go*. Or *Fodor's*. Either way, it was cool as all hell. She half expected a Beefeater to come marching by.

"Are you ready, then?" Zoe slid down off the lion.

"Yeah, um, will you just take my picture? In front of the lions?" Abby asked, handing her digital camera over.

"Sure thing, sister. Closer to the right. Not that close," Zoe commanded, waving.

"Okay, this is it. You look bee-yoo-ti-ful. Smile."

She put the camera down and placed her hand on her hip in frustration. "Excuse me, but do you have some form of clinical depression? Seasonal Affective Disorder, or something? Because where I come from, that's not a smile, that's indigestion."

Abby burst out laughing.

"Yes, much better." Zoe raised the camera again. "Now say . . ."A smile of her own spread across her face. "Say 'Westminster' *Abby*!"

"Westminster *Abby*!"

For Caroline, for braving the hall bar, the dining halls, the West End, and the rest of Western Europe with me when we were mates back at City University (such a bad influence you were!). And for letting me star in all of your stories from our time in London.

SPEAK
Published by the Penguin Group
Penguin Group (USA) Inc.,
345 Hudson Street, New York, New York 10014, U.S.A.
Penguin Group (Canada), 10 Alcorn Avenue, Toronto, Ontario, Canada M4V 3B2
(a division of Pearson Penguin Canada Inc.)
Penguin Books Ltd, 80 Strand, London WC2R 0RL, England
Penguin Ireland, 25 St Stephen's Green, Dublin 2, Ireland
(a division of Penguin Books Ltd)
Penguin Group (Australia), 250 Camberwell Road, Camberwell, Victoria 3124, Australia
(a division of Pearson Australia Group Pty Ltd)
Penguin Books India Pvt Ltd, 11 Community Centre, Panchsheel Park,
New Delhi - 110 017, India
Penguin Group (NZ), Cnr Airborne and Rosedale Roads, Albany, Auckland 1310,
New Zealand (a division of Pearson New Zealand Ltd)
Penguin Books (South Africa) (Pty) Ltd, 24 Sturdee Avenue, Rosebank, Johannesburg 2196,
South Africa

Registered Offices: Penguin Books Ltd, 80 Strand, London WC2R 0RL, England

Published by Speak, an imprint of Penguin Group (USA) Inc., 2005

5 7 9 10 8 6

Copyright © Micol Ostow, 2005
All rights reserved
Interior art and design by Jeanine Henderson. Text set in Imago Book.

ISBN 978-0-14-240413-3

Printed in the United States of America

S.A.S.S.
STUDENTS ACROSS THE SEVEN SEAS

Westminster Abby

Micol Ostow

speak
An Imprint of Penguin Group (USA) Inc.

Abby's London

City University/Finsbury Hall

St. Paul's Cathedral

Tower Bridge

Big Ben

Thames River

Tate Modern

Millennium Eye

Application
Students Across the Seven Seas Study Abroad Program

Name: Abby Capshaw

Age: 16

High School: Hamilton School of Upper Manhattan

Hometown: New York City

Preferred Study Abroad Destination: London, England

1. Why are you interested in traveling abroad next year?

Answer: I'd like to enrich my high school academic experience by challenging myself to take college-level courses, and to expand upon my personal growth by studying in a foreign country.

(Truth: Actually, I wasn't the one who wanted to travel abroad in the first place. This was all my parents' idea—but I'm beginning to think it's not such a bad one.)

2. How will studying abroad further develop your talents and interests?

Answer: English and writing are especially appealing to me, and I hope that my experiences in England would deepen those interests.

(Truth: I'll be thousands of miles away from home, so I might actually be able to have some fun that doesn't entail playing Boggle with the 'rents.)

3. Describe your extracurricular activities.

Answer: Hamilton Peer-to-Peer Program Tutor, Alpha Zeta Honors Society, Member of Future Leaders of America

(Truth: Not much to report. My parents only approve weekend outings that include a sleepover at my best friend Dani's house.)

4. Is there anything else you feel we should know about you?

Answer: I'm responsible and focused, and I'm confident that I'd excel in finding a balance between exploring a foreign country and doing well in my classes.

(Truth: I can't wait to spice up my life with a little British influence.)

Chapter One

"In the event of an emergency, a member of the flight crew shall direct you to the nearest exit."

Abby Capshaw shifted nervously in the narrow confines of her tiny window seat. One of these days, she vowed to herself, when she was long past high school and making an actual salary instead of a paltry allowance and some money from babysitting, she was going to spring for a first-class ride. The plane had taken off, like, three seconds ago, and already her knees were cramping.

Normally Abby would be paying attention to the announcements that the captain was making over the

loudspeaker, or craning her neck to see the flight crew's safety demonstration. She was a firm believer that one never could be too cautious—she'd seen *Castaway*. It was important to be prepared. And Abby was nothing if not the responsible type. She was spacing now for two very specific reasons.

For starters, she couldn't understand a word that the captain was saying. She knew he was speaking in English because this was a British Airways flight and, well, he *was* English, but she had quickly discovered—with no small amount of dismay—that apparently a British accent was actually kind of tough to decipher in any context other than a Hugh Grant movie. Since boarding Flight 0178 to London's Heathrow Airport, Abby had found herself doing more politely ambiguous nodding than she had, pretty much, ever done in her whole life (family reunions notwithstanding).

So listening to the captain was essentially an exercise in futility. Though she did note with some amusement that he pronounced *direct* as "die-rect."

Just like Hugh Grant. Mmmm...

The other reason that Abby was slightly less concerned than usual about hearing the announcements had to do with why she was on this plane to begin with: the whole "responsible type" thing. As in, she was tired of it. And she was looking for a change. Starting now.

Abby's junior year of high school had begun with a vow:

Things were going to be different this year. Last fall, on September 13, Abby had turned sixteen. She was a Virgo. Normally she didn't pay all that much attention to things like horoscopes and the zodiac, but her best friend, Dani Schumacher, was a huge believer in it, and, as such, kept Abby well informed on the subject.

According to *Who Do the Stars Think You Are?* (a dubious source, in Abby's humble opinion), being a Virgo meant that Abby was "a hardworking, dedicated personality who wants perfection in all you do. Because you are very organized, you make the perfect party planner!"

In other words, totally boring. (Except for that party-planner thing, which didn't so much apply to her life. Though one time her principal asked her to put together a casual going-away thing for her English teacher. But there was nothing sexy about a party your principal asked you to plan.)

Abby had to admit to herself that life in New York City was pretty much okay. She went to a nice private school where the kids were decent and down-to-earth, even though most of them had a lot of money—definitely more money than she had (well, technically, more than her parents). She got very good grades and tutored through a peer-to-peer program. She had a small, close-knit circle of friends. Maybe she wasn't captain of the cheerleading squad or anything like that, but she fit in and felt well liked.

Terminally boring.

She had discovered that she was a little vanilla. Actually, way more than a little. She needed some flavor. Some hot fudge or colored sprinkles. Ideally, she could spin "vanilla" into "hot fudge sundae." The goal had been to put the plan into action over the course of junior year. But things hadn't quite worked out the way Abby'd planned.

Her parents were completely overprotective of her (not that she'd ever given them reason to be—so unfair), making her stay home most Friday nights for "family time" and forbidding her to date until she was seventeen. Seventeen was ancient. Seventeen was *senior* year. By then, everyone in school would have paired off and she'd be lucky to go to the prom with her cousin Jeff. Clearly that was out of the question. Things had to change, and fast.

"Biscuits?"

Abby felt a tap at her arm and looked up to see a cheery blond flight attendant beaming away at her. "Huh?" she asked.

"Biscuits, luv. A package."

Abby peered at the plastic package, trying to decipher what was inside. It was definitely something of the edible variety, that much was for sure, but as a general rule, she liked to have a vague sense of what she was eating before she dove in. Then again, she *was* sort of hungry. She nodded and took the snack. If nothing else, it was a crash course in British culture.

"Something to drink?"

Abby shrugged. "Water?"

"Certainly. Fizzy or still?"

"Um...tap. Plain. I mean, still," Abby stammered. The flight attendant passed a small chilled bottle across the row. Abby took her drink and placed it down on her tray, then ripped open the package of biscuits.

Oh! Biscuits were cookies. These were plain and flat, and cream-colored, probably vanilla-flavored. Not very exciting. Kind of like Abby's life. How appropriate.

She mentally flipped through the glossary she'd been sent from her program director before leaving: *bird, biscuit, bloke, boot, brolly, chemist, jumper, knickers, lorry, loo, newsagent, pants, trainers, WC*—the words were either completely foreign, or familiar, but with a totally different meaning. For instance, she'd been warned not to use the word *pants* to mean "trousers" because in England, pants were underwear. Like *knickers*. Knickers were also under-wear. Totally confusing.

Abby didn't care—that much—though, because being in this cramped, crowded plane and navigating her way through secret, coded language and pseudoexotic snacks was the first step toward that hot-fudge-sundae lifestyle she so craved. She was on her way to London. To *live*.

A thrill ran through her just thinking about it. She'd been accepted to the S.A.S.S. program—a program that encouraged high-school girls to study abroad—then she'd

been approved for admittance to City College, a university based in the eastern area of the city, for a ten-week summer session. Ten weeks. In London, one of the most cosmopolitan cities in the world. London was all about cool, sophisticated accents, fancy meals like "high tea," live theater that rivaled Broadway, actual royalty complete with palaces and everything—and she'd be right in the middle of it.

Was she scared? No way.

She was terrified.

The most ironic part about the trip was that the whole thing had been her parents' idea in the first place. *They* had been the ones who'd found the S.A.S.S. program and decided that it sounded like "an opportunity not to be missed." *They* had been the ones who *insisted* that Abby apply. The same people who got on Abby when she received an A-minus rather than an A on a paper or a test (which for the record, was pretty damn rare). The same people who acted shocked when Abby professed a desire to see a movie with her friends rather than play Boggle on family night. It was these two people who had driven Abby to elaborate measures of faux rebellion such as talking on her phone from inside her bedroom closet when it was later than 10 P.M., her "phone curfew." *Those people* actually *wanted her to move to England. For ten whole weeks.*

Ultimately, Abby's reasons for wanting to stay and her parents' *highly* uncharacteristic reasons for wanting to ship her off to a different time zone were one and the same. One reason, to be precise. A boy reason.

A boy named James.

Back in November, Abby would have given anything not to be separated from James, which was obviously why her parents had insisted on doing just that. They pulled out that "not until you're seventeen" bull, which Abby was pretty sure they'd made up on the spot just because she'd happened to take an interest in the opposite sex. She was too young to date, they proclaimed, but paradoxically, she was old enough to be thrown to the proverbial wolves for the summer. The British wolves.

Abby had used every tactic she could possibly conceive of: She cried, begged, pleaded, suffered weeks without talking to her parents or eating (in their presence, anyway)...to no effect. Abby loved James, James was bad news, Abby was going to England.

At the eleventh hour, Abby had finally come to terms with the tragic situation and used her rather prodigious babysitting savings to buy James a plane ticket over to England to visit her halfway through the summer term. There was *no way* that she was going to spend the entire summer apart from the boy she loved.

It was funny how things could change so dramatically, so quickly, Abby thought.

She took a sip of her water and broke off a tiny piece of her biscuit. It was hard and bland, like one might expect of

a cookie that was called a "digestive." It tasted of vanilla—chalky, gritty vanilla.

But that was okay.

Because in seven hours—*wait, no, six and a half,* she realized, glancing at her watch—Abby's whole world was going to be a giant, gooey pint of New York Superfudge Chunk.

Well, except in London, of course.

Chapter Two

The country that once determined the meaning of civilised *now takes many of its cultural cues from former fledgling colonies. The vanguard of art, music, film, and eclecticism, England is a youthful, hip nation looking forward. But traditionalists can rest easy; for all the moving and shaking in the large cities, around the corner there are quaint towns, dozens of picturesque castles, and scores of comforting cups of tea.*

As the plane taxied along the runway, Abby reluctantly stashed her guidebook in her tote bag. From her post at

the window, the landscape looked basically like any other. It was late, almost nine at night, and still, somehow, the sky overhead was gray and overcast. She'd been warned about the weather in England, about how rare an occurrence a sunny day would be. She had hoped those warnings were exaggerated, but she was starting to suspect that perhaps they were not.

She followed the crush of deboarding passengers, and hopped on a small shuttle that, with any luck, would take her to the main terminals at Heathrow.

"It's going to be a horrible queue," a man said to his wife. "Everyone coming back from summer holidays all at once." In her head Abby translated, *It's going to be a long line, with everyone coming back from vacation.* The baggage-claim line, she supposed. Or the line for a taxi. All the lines, for that matter. Her neighbor was also soft, round, and somewhat pale, as many of the middle-aged folks in the car seemed to be. Coming from New York City, Abby was used to a more diverse crowd on the subways and public transportation, and certainly many more ethnic-looking folk with darker hair and darker complexions. Though she did notice quite a few Indians and Southeast Asians on the shuttle, which she knew was the norm in London.

And if the middle-aged shuttle riders all smacked of a certain station in life and a corresponding "look," so, too, did the younger urbanites. She saw a lot of slim black pants, eyeliner (on the women), and heels. Even though it was summer, it wasn't nearly as warm as it got in New York City, and most people here at least carried some long-sleeve layers with them. She saw businessmen, thin and sun-deprived, their suits rumpled from hard travel. There were also a few teens who looked like punk-rock refugees, decked out with heavy jewelry, shapeless black T-shirts pulled tightly over stretched-out thermals, thick boots, and sullen expressions. Abby imagined this shuttle car to be a microcosmic representation of the country.

It didn't bode well that she could barely make out a word anyone was saying.

After she had located her enormous backpack and duffel from baggage claim, Abby made her way to the customs area. From there she was supposed to meet Reuben, her program director, who would accompany her in a taxi over to the school.

Abby wove her way through the maze of airport chain stores and restaurants, past a few quickie sandwich stops like Pret A Manger and Boots, which looked a lot like a British Rite Aid or CVS. The airport itself didn't seem all that different from JFK, save for an outpost of Harrods department store just outside the duty-free area and a bill-board advertisement that suggested A CUPPA WHILST YOU WAIT FOR YOUR FLIGHT.

Finally Abby came upon the central waiting area on the

far side of the baggage claim. Immediately she noticed a tall, stout middle-aged man with thick, graying black hair and a salt-and-pepper beard. He was wearing a City College T-shirt and jeans. This could only be Reuben. Spotting Abby, he waved and beckoned her over to him.

"Hello!" he boomed at her. Abby was relieved to hear his American accent. He clapped her on the back with one hand and, with the other, gestured for her to hand over her luggage, which she did gratefully. "You must be Abby!"

"How can you tell?" she asked.

"Well, for starters, most of the other Americans arrived on the earlier flight. But more specifically, because your mother called me in advance and described to me what you are wearing. Not to mention I had that photo that she sent," he explained.

Abby blushed. "Yeah, she's...thorough," she said. "Remind me to call her later." Her parents had bought her a special international cell phone for her trip and had established Sundays as "check-in" day. But Abby knew if she waited until Sunday to let her parents know she'd gotten in safely, she'd be toast.

Reuben laughed. "Somehow, I have a feeling you won't be able to forget." He led Abby outside to where a string of black cabs were parked and lined up in a long row. Abby had to laugh as the driver of their cab emerged from what would have been the passenger side of the car (in the states, anyway) to let them in.

The ride to school would take around an hour, Reuben said, since there wouldn't be much traffic on a Thursday night. He took the opportunity in the cab to talk about what Abby could expect at City, as well as to lay out some ground rules of her dorm, Finsbury Hall. Reuben himself served as a student liaison at the school. He lived in a "flat" nearby and was available all day for any crises, emergencies, or even just plain old questions.

"Your mother asked that I give her weekly updates on your progress at City," Reuben offered cautiously, after he'd run through the basics of the program. Abby rolled her eyes but didn't say anything.

"I take it that doesn't surprise you?" he commented.

Abby shrugged. Her parents were control freaks, big-time. Nothing they did would surprise her. That was why she'd agreed to come to London, finally. To be on her own and try to shake things up.

Abby wasn't the only one who'd been interested in shaking things up during junior year. Her best friend, Dani, had also decided that at age sixteen, the two girls were ready to let loose. By Abby's standards, Dani had been letting loose basically since the sixth grade, but given how Abby both needed and wanted Dani as a partner in crime, she didn't see the point in quibbling.

One of the key differences between Dani and Abby was that while Abby was a thinker, Dani was without a doubt a

doer. Dani thought it had to do with the fact that she was an Aries, a fire sign who was—according again to *Who Do the Stars Think You Are?*—"a natural-born leader! You are up for challenges and ready to sink all of your energy into whatever piques your interest."

Again, Abby wasn't sure what she thought of the whole zodiac thing, but it did seem to have a positive influence on Dani, at least in the sense of motivating her.

Dani's grand idea junior year had come to her in a flash, she later told Abby, during an especially moving episode of *The O.C.* Since Abby's television viewing, like everything else in her life, was heavily monitored, she hadn't caught this particular episode, but the way Dani described it, the main characters had all gone wild at some college party.

"That's what we need," Dani had told Abby over a lunch of frozen yogurt in the school cafeteria.

"TiVo?" Abby asked, confused. "At least you could tape the episodes for me, you know."

Dani sighed, pushing her empty yogurt cup away. "No, loser. A party. A *college* party."

Abby laughed. "Right. That'll happen. It's hard enough convincing my parents to let me stay at your place overnight."

"Yeah, but they always give in, in the end, don't they?" Dani pointed out.

"For me to stay at your house? Sure. They know you.

They've known you since I was in the first grade. You are not a scary college party."

Dani rolled her eyes. "Work with me, please, friend." She leaned forward. "Spencer has some friends who just pledged Zeta Omega." Spencer was Dani's older brother. He was a freshman at NYU and lived in the dorms downtown.

"And?" Abby asked.

"And they're all having a party on induction night. An off-campus party at this bar downtown. Spencer swears the place never cards."

Now Abby put her yogurt down to give her friend her full attention. "I sincerely hope you're not suggesting that we go to this party? Or do I need to redirect you to Exhibit A, wherein my parents *do not let me engage in social activities that are not either school-sanctioned, or taking place at your house.*"

Dani sighed heavily. "Which is why you are going to tell them that you're staying at my place," she said.

Abby stared at her friend. "You're asking me to lie to my parents?"

"I'm *telling* you to lie to your parents," Dani clarified. "There's no room for negotiation here."

Abby shook her head definitively. "It's never going to work."

"Of *course* it's going to work," Dani insisted. "When, in the history of your teenage life, have you ever lied to them?"

"Never," Abby said.

"Exactly. So they have no reason *not* to believe you, right?"

Abby paused. Dani had a point. This was probably something that they would be able to get away with. But did that mean that they *should*? Sure, her parents were insanely controlling, and sure, Abby was sick and tired of feeling like her social life was under lock and key, but still... she'd never outright *lied* to them before, and she didn't really see herself as the kind of person who did stuff like that. Dishonest stuff.

Dani leaned forward and grabbed Abby's hand. "This is not a criminal offense, Abby. This is a small white lie. *Tiny.* One that may be *crucial* to the development of your social life. You wanted things to change. What were you thinking, you'd get a nipple ring?"

Abby winced at the visual image.

"Exactly," Dani said. "This is way more benign than that. It's just a little fun for a night."

Abby shrugged. She was tempted, no doubt about it. But that didn't change the basic facts. "We'll never get away with it," she told Dani. "No way."

"And you said we'd never get away with it," Dani said, smirking and clutching a bottle of Amstel Light like the precious cargo that it was.

"What can I say?" Abby responded, happily sipping at her own bottle of beer. "I was wrong. It's been known to happen."

"I *love* the fact that your parents think we're having a sleepover," Dani said, giggling.

"And *I* love that your parents think we're at a concert. I mean, don't they know that Spencer's not in a band?"

"I hear my name being called. Does this mean you're talking trash about me?" Spencer sidled up to his sister and wrapped one arm around her affably.

"Spence, what instrument do you play?" Dani asked.

"Oh, in the imaginary world? Bass. I'm hell at the bass." Spencer laughed. "Let me guess: You told Mom and Dad that you wanted to hear my 'band' play tonight."

"One of these days, you're going to have to actually buy a guitar or something, Spencer, or they're going to get suspicious," Abby said, winking at him.

"Always the practical one," Spencer joked, reaching out to tug at one of Abby's braids.

"Doesn't she look cute?" Dani asked, pointing to the braided pigtails. "I practically had to pay her to agree to let me do them."

"I look like I'm five," Abby complained. "Especially with this stupid tank top you picked out." She pointed at the tiny Winnie-the-Pooh centered on the front of her shirt. "He's, like, announcing my flat-chestedness to the whole room."

"He's announcing your foxiness to my friend, actually," Spencer interjected. "That's kind of why I came over."

"What? Who? How?" Abby asked, nearly spilling her drink all over Winnie. Which was probably for the best. She'd really never drunk before, other than a glass of champagne at her cousin's wedding, and she was starting to feel a little bit fuzzy-headed after one half of a light beer.

Spencer jerked his head to the left and behind him, where a tall, thin boy was lazily leaning against the jukebox. He wore a Wheaties-logo T-shirt, baggy jeans, and Vans. There was some definite use of product going on in his thick, curly hair. He didn't look anything like a frat boy. In fact, to Abby, he looked like a member of Spencer's band. If Spencer's band had, you know, actually existed. When Wheaties caught Abby checking him out, he grinned.

"Oh!" Abby whirled, repositioning herself so that she was no longer Winnie-to-Wheaties.

"Excuse me, but that guy is *hot*," Dani said. "Can you please explain to me what you're doing turning your back to him?"

"Not my back, my shoulder," Abby reasoned. "Why? What am I supposed to do, go *talk* to him?" Her eyes widened in panic at the thought.

"Um, yes, actually. That would be the first step in this process we call flirting," Dani said drily.

"But—I mean, I don't talk to boys," Abby stammered.

"You talk to me," Spencer pointed out.

"You're not a boy!" Abby exclaimed. "You're, like, almost my older brother. Please. It's not the same at all."

"Thanks," Spencer said, pretending to be offended.

"Besides, what could I ever talk to him about?" she asked.

"The fact that you're both wearing dumb T-shirts that you're pretending came from a thrift shop but really came straight from Urban Outfitters," Dani suggested.

"This is *your* shirt!" Abby said.

"He's not a serial killer," Spencer said. "He's an English major. And a really good writer, too. We have a workshop together."

"It's just a conversation, Abby," Dani pointed out. "With a cute college boy. No one's asking you to have his children or even go out with him. Just go over and say hello. No wait—don't."

"Huh?" Abby had just placed her beer down at the edge of the bar, finally feeling slightly emboldened. "But you said—"

"I know what I said. Now shut up and look cute."

"I—how? Okay," Abby said, putting her hands on her hips, then folding them across her chest, and finally settling for hooking her thumbs into her jeans pocket.

When she finally looked up, she realized why Dani had commanded the cuteness.

Standing before her was the boy from the jukebox. Wheaties. The English major. The wannabe retro kid. The would-be rock star.

"Hi," he said, his entire body seeming to smile at her. "I'm James."

Chapter Three

Abby sat up in bed and promptly hit her head on the corner of an overhead shelf. "Ow," she grumbled, rubbing at the bump. Since when was there a shelf above her bed? She leaned forward and peered out the window. The soaring towers of St. Paul's Cathedral waved to her.

Oh. Right.

She was in London.

She'd arrived with Reuben at eleven the night before and had promptly been indoctrinated when the elevator had jammed on her unceremoniously. Nice. She'd been

halfway between the eighth and ninth floors when the machine just stopped moving. There was nothing quite like unintelligible Cockney English being screeched through an air shaft at top volume. *"Ang on, luv, we'll have you out of 'ere in a jiff! Won't be but a mo'!"* The thick intonation was rendered all the more indecipherable by the heavy hiss of static running through the intercom system. Highly soothing—*not.*

"S'okay," Abby had responded, miserable (could they even hear her? Did the intercom go both ways?), slumped on the floor, surrounded by her S.A.S.S. welcome packet and City College welcome brochures written in incongruously cheery rhetoric. "You may be unaccustomed to the plumbing in the United Kingdom, but have patience!"

Very promising. She wondered if Mara, her friend from home who was studying abroad in Florence, would have to deal with plumbing issues, too.

Once Abby'd been rescued, she'd fished her toothbrush out of her carry-on bag, washed her face, and crawled into her tiny single bed in her tiny single room on the ninth floor, suitcases and all thoughts of organization abandoned for the evening.

But this morning, the Nice Girl at heart couldn't bear being surrounded by bags taller than her person and shirts strewn across the floor instead of neatly folded in drawers or stacked precisely on shelves. Even if she'd promised herself that this trip was going to be a chance to break out of her usual routine, terminal neat-itude was, like, deeply ingrained. And not knowing exactly when she'd get organized was starting to grate at her last nerve.

But she couldn't unpack now, anyway, or she'd be late for breakfast and orientation.

Abby fished through her duffel until she located the components of a reasonably acceptable outfit: clean jeans, a black tank top, and a pair of open-toed shoes, and shimmied into her clothing. A brush through the hair and a swipe of lip gloss and she was ready. Sort of. Never mind that it was three in the morning back in the U.S. She consulted her orientation schedule.

Saturday, 4 June

8 A.M.: Breakfast, Finsbury Hall dining room

9 A.M.: Orientation lecture, Finsbury Hall lounge

10 A.M.: Campus Tour

11 A.M.-4 P.M.: Tour of West End (buses to depart from in front of Finsbury Hall)

•Parliament

•Big Ben

•Westminster Abbey

•Trafalgar Square

4-6 P.M.: free

6 P.M.: early dinner (meet on stairs of National Portrait Gallery)

8 P.M.: *Oliver!* (smart dress)

The thought of having two free hours in the middle of the afternoon was terrifying to Abby. She hadn't met a soul from her dorms just yet. She was going to have to push her inherent shyness aside and somehow make a friend.

Or—if that proved to be too much of a challenge—at the very least, an acquaintance.

Breakfast was a dismal affair: The dining hall was a small, dreary space half the size of her high-school cafeteria, set apart by several rows of long, institution-style tables and a short steam tray along the back wall. Abby found an odd array of choices: eggs; thick, greasy bacon; and, strangely, lumpy pools of baked beans. One tray over she found a mountain of deep-fried Tater Tots smiling up at her. (Literally. They were cut in the shape of little smiley faces. So weird.) Abby passed on the hot food and poured herself a bowl of generic cornflakes. She doused her cereal in whole milk, balanced a glass of suspiciously watery OJ on her tray, and carefully maneuvered herself over to the tables.

The sea of unfamiliar faces caused her no small amount of panic. The number of people Abby didn't know in this room was far greater than the number of people she *did* know, cumulative, back home. And even if she hadn't been Miss Popularity back at the Hamilton School of Upper Manhattan, at least she'd never felt overtly uncomfortable among her classmates. They'd all been in school together for far too long for that. She glanced around, seeing one other girl also sitting alone. This girl had thick stripes of bright green hair interspersed among her chin-length brown bob and a ring on every finger—not to mention one in her nose. She was wearing a pink short-sleeve Atari-logo T-shirt over a tighter black T-shirt. She didn't seem at all fazed to be sitting by herself, and Abby briefly wondered if other people were sort of afraid to sit down next to her—she looked a bit intimidating, what with the flaming green hair and all. Abby couldn't imagine that she and this girl would have all that much in common. But it beat eating alone.

Reminding herself of how much she had wanted a challenge and some change in her life, Abby took a deep breath, crossed the room, and slid into the seat across from Atari.

"No happy-face potatoes?" Atari asked her. "I really thought they were the only edible choice."

Abby shrugged. "Cereal seemed safe."

"Whole milk makes me want to yak," Atari said.

"Well, I have some Lactaid back in my room," Abby offered. "My mom packed it for me. She thinks they don't have drugstores in England."

Atari paused, peering at Abby as though debating whether or not she was being sincere. Abby suddenly felt self-conscious, like she'd maybe forgotten to put her clothes on over her underwear. Clearly, referencing lactose intolerance was severely uncool, and Abby briefly prayed

that she would be sucked into the ground underneath their table and never again have to show her face in the dining hall.

After a moment, though, Atari burst into laughter, evidently having decided that Abby was kidding—and, fortunately, that she liked the joke.

"Awesome, I'll keep that in mind," she said. "I'm Zoe."

"I'm Abby. Capshaw," Abby said. She thought about holding her hand out for a shake but thought better of it as Zoe slurped Tater Tot residue from her fingers. "I'm from New York."

"Really? I'm from Philly. Are you here with S.A.S.S.?"

Abby nodded.

"How cool is it that our high schools have S.A.S.S. exchange programs?" Zoe asked.

"Well, to be honest, I was really nervous about coming abroad," Abby hedged. She saw Zoe's eyes widen in disbelief and quickly changed tacks. "But yeah, totally cool," she finished, deciding that it was all a question of mind over matter.

It had to be—didn't it?

The Finsbury Hall lounge turned out to be only slightly less depressing than the dining hall. The room was small and smelled of smoke. One uncomfortable-looking couch lay along the back wall, flanked by two equally uninviting love seats. Every available surface area was occupied by the time Zoe and Abby had finished their breakfast. Abby had another of her increasingly common momentary heart attacks and envisioned the entire room staring directly at her as she stood throughout the orientation lecture. Zoe, on the other hand, seemed thoroughly undaunted. "I guess we have to squat," she pronounced, after casing the joint rather cursorily. She slid down and crossed her legs school-style, patting the floor next to her in an invitation for which Abby was wholly grateful.

Abby arranged herself on the ground next to Zoe. Zoe leaned in. "That's Simon," she said, motioning to a tall, lanky, bored-looking boy sprawled against the edge of a love seat. She winked at him and he nodded back. "He's from Ireland. And there's Chrissy." She pointed to a stout blonde looking beatific in a long, flowy skirt. "She's a S.A.S.S.-program chick, too, and from Georgia, and that's Fred from Portugal."

Abby's head spun. Zoe had only come in a few hours earlier than Abby had—how had she had the time to meet all of these people? Suddenly it seemed that Abby had somehow missed the secret induction ceremony. Thank God Zoe seemed perfectly happy to help bring her up to speed.

Before Abby could respond to Zoe's Who's Who of Finsbury Hall tutorial, the door to the lounge swung open and in strode Reuben.

"Hello!" he boomed, his thick beard bobbing up and down with every syllable. "I trust you're all well rested and not at all jet-lagged?" His eyes twinkled as though he genuinely believed this to be a riotous joke. Zoe turned to Abby and rolled her eyes.

"First things first," he continued. "Your schedules. You should all have preregistered for your courses back home, no?" He paused, allowing for a dutiful if unenthused wave of student nodding. "In which case, on Monday, you'll report to the office of international students first thing, where you'll be given a printout of your schedules."

"Where—" began one anxious-looking redhead seated at the foot of the couch.

"I have maps of the campus that I will be distributing, in addition to the tour that will directly follow this meeting," Reuben said.

"Now then. Meals. Meals are served three times a day—the exact times are posted outside of the dining hall, which you may have noticed this morning."

"I was lucky just to *find* the dining hall this morning," Zoe stage-whispered, eliciting a chorus of giggles from the nearby students and a glare of mock disapproval from Reuben. "I am *useless* without my coffee."

"On Saturdays and Sundays, however, only two meals are served," Reuben continued, pointedly ignoring Zoe. "A brunch, and then dinner. But I'm sure many of you will want to go elsewhere on weekend evenings for dinner.

"You've been given your room keys. On Monday you'll need to report to the student affairs office and get your photos taken for your ID cards, as well. After this weekend, those IDs will be required to gain access to the building. You will be permitted to have guests—who will have to sign in with photo ID as well—provided that you clear it with me in writing beforehand.

"The night watchman will have access to all emergency numbers, should you need them, and we have e-mail terminals and laundry service in the basement. The cleaners come by once a day to clean the bathrooms and common areas. They will clean your individual rooms once a week. The only other piece of advice I can give you is that you should probably go easy on the hall bar until you get your sea legs." He grinned at them knowingly.

Hall bar? Like, a bar in the hall? Abby wondered fleetingly. Of course everyone in New York City could get into bars if and when they wanted to—she'd certainly experienced that firsthand, tagging along with James (while her parents thought she was at Dani's)—but this seemed different. To have one in the dorms? Surely that was a disaster waiting to happen.

Abby surveyed the faces of her fellow dorm mates. Chrissy from Georgia didn't look the least bit anxious about coping with the hedonistic lures of a hall bar. Fred from

Portugal, in fact, looked downright pleased about it. Zoe looked incredibly bored. She was twisting a thick chunk of green hair around her finger until it hung in a Shirley Temple–style ringlet. She caught Abby staring and stuck her tongue out. It was pierced, naturally.

Zoe raised her hand and leaned forward on the carpet. "Reuben? Reuben? Reuben?" she asked, sounding like an impatient three-year-old.

Reuben was completely unflappable. Abby realized that, as a program director, he was probably pretty good at assessing his students' characters early on. Not to mention that, in his job, he'd probably seen worse. "Yes?" he asked. "Before you pop a vein, dear."

Zoe jerked her head in Abby's direction. "Abby wants to know when we're leaving for the West End." She gave Abby a playful shove, nearly sending her over.

What felt like a thousand pairs of eyes turned and trained themselves on Abby. She concentrated on making herself very very small. It didn't seem to have much effect.

What the hell? she decided. Reuben didn't look at all annoyed. If anything, he seemed entertained by Zoe—not that Abby blamed him. Zoe was definitely different from any of her friends back home. She was even different from Dani, who of course wasn't the least bit shy. But wasn't different good? Wasn't different, like, the whole point?

Under normal circumstances, Abby would have prayed

to the Gods of Bad Timing to make her disappear without a trace. But these weren't normal circumstances. These weren't her friends, classmates, or teachers from back home. Here she could be anything she wanted to. Less "responsible." Less "mature." Less of a goody-goody.

She shrugged, smiling guiltily. "I've never been there before."

"The city of Westminster, now a borough of London, has been the seat of British power for over a thousand years. William the Conqueror was crowned in Westminster Abbey on Christmas Day, 1066, and his successors built the palace of Westminster that would one day house Parliament."

"Abby, you freak, put down the guidebook and come see this!"

Abby reluctantly folded the page of her book as a placeholder and wandered to where Zoe was standing with Chrissy, Fred, and Simon. The group was examining a series of stained-glass windows in the north transept along with the rest of the students. Reuben had arranged for a special tour, but Abby still felt compelled to sneak intermittent glances at her guidebook.

"It's very sad, how devoted you are to that book," Zoe commented. "I'm thinking you never had a pet growing up?"

Abby laughed. "Fair enough. But how else would you have understood the subtle differences between the North

Rose Window, the John Bunyon Window, and the HMS Captain Window?"

"How about we just play it by ear?" Chrissy asked.

Abby's eyebrows shot up. "I'm not very good at that," she confessed.

"Just follow our lead, Abby," Simon said, patting her on the back.

Zoe linked arms with Abby and gave her a playful nudge. "Yes, and try to say good-bye to the Abbey. Now's time to break out on our own, *chica*!"

"What was that book? With the birds? In Trafalgar Square?" Zoe called out to Abby. "You know, and that crazy woman was feeding them?"

Zoe had scaled the staircase of Trafalgar Square and was snuggling up to one of the two enormous bronze lions that flanked the staircase. She was shaking her hips rather exuberantly and calling to the flocks of pigeons scattered on the landing below. Simon, Chrissy, and Fred were mugging for Fred's digital camera over on the opposite side of the square.

"*Mary Poppins*?"

"Yes! How did I guess you would know?" Zoe grinned at her. You are so obviously a book person."

"And you're not," Abby guessed, hoping she sounded more curious than snobby. Green hair or no, after she'd spent the day with Zoe, it was clear the girl was anything but dim.

"Well, I'm not necessarily into walking through the streets of London with my face planted in a copy of *Lonely Planet*, that's for sure," Zoe teased.

"It's *Fodor's*—" Abby interjected.

"Whatever. I like comics, graphic novels, manga, you know. That kind of stuff."

"Well, uh, I don't think that *Lonely Planet* has a line of graphic-novel guidebooks," Abby said.

Zoe snorted. "Touché, my friend. But you're missing the point. And more importantly, you're so busy with that stupid book that you're missing out on all of the actual sights!"

"Not true!" Abby protested.

"Look!" Zoe tilted Abby's head toward the direction of the Thames. "It's Big Ben. How many times have you seen that sucker on a postcard? And it's right there in front of you, for real. Are you even noticing?"

"I am," Abby said. "And as a matter of fact, that's not Big Ben, that's the Parliament Clock Tower. Big Ben is actually the bell inside. It's named after Sir Benjamin Hall, who served as commissioner of works when the bell was cast in 1858."

Zoe looked at Abby. "Is this some sort of cry for help? I mean, you're practically *begging* me to toss that thing right into the river."

"You'd never make it from here," Abby said, squaring off against her new friend.

Zoe burst out laughing. "Yeah, I throw like a girl."

"It *is* cool, though," Abby said. And it was. The soaring architecture of Parliament and Big Ben were truly a testimony to an era gone by. The imposing building was framed neatly by the sky—as gray as it was—and stood in stark, rich contrast to the shimmering river. She was glad she had paid attention in history class; this place just had so *much* of it. Standing in the center of the square, she could imagine herself, first as one of the politicians to sit in the Houses of Parliament, and then as a religious leader buried beneath the Abbey, and finally, as a character straight out of children's literature. Maybe Zoe had the right idea with her pigeon reference.

The whole place just seemed so…*British*. There was no other word for it. It wasn't exotic in the way that she imagined the Far East would be. It wasn't idyllic like a Caribbean island. In fact, it was just as dank and gray as she'd been promised. And yet, expansive, colorless, and understated as London seemed, it was, to Abby, completely alive. She was living her *Let's Go*. Or *Fodor's*. Either way, it was cool as all hell. She half expected a Beefeater to come marching by.

"When do you think we're going to see Buckingham Palace?" she wondered aloud.

Zoe shrugged and checked her watch. "It's quarter to four. We have from four to six free. We could probably squeeze it in today if we wanted to, but I think that might be overkill. I mean, we've been touring for hours already. We have a whole summer here. We can just do it next weekend or whatever. Wouldn't you rather do it on a day when you're fresh, when you can appreciate it?"

"Sure," Abby said, pleased at the thought of hanging out with Zoe on a regular basis.

"Good, then it's settled," Zoe said. "Those guys"—she indicated their friends, now grinning cross-eyed into the camera as Simon held it inches away from their face— "were saying we should all go for a drink before dinner."

"What? Oh, I mean, cool!" Abby said, flustered.

"Are you ready, then?" Zoe slid down off the lion and gave a final shake of her butt toward the pigeons, who responded by exploding into a frenzy of flapping wings.

"Yeah, um, will you just take my picture? In front of the lions?" Abby asked, handing her digital camera over. "You just have to press that button."

"Sure thing, sister. Closer to the right. Not that close," Zoe commanded, waving. "Cool. I want to get some pigeons into the frame."

"You scared them all away with your disco trip," Abby pointed out.

"Well, sure, if you're going to be all nitpicky about it.

Okay, this is it. You look bee-yoo-ti-ful. Smile."

She put the camera down and placed her hand on her hip in frustration. "Excuse me, but do you have some form of clinical depression? Seasonal Affective Disorder, or something? Because where I come from, that's not a smile, that's indigestion."

Abby burst out laughing.

"Yes, much better." Zoe raised the camera again. "Now say..." A smile of her own spread across her face. "Say 'Westminster' *Abby*!"

"Westminster *Abby*!"

"What'll it be?" Simon asked, rising from his worn, oversize armchair.

"Uh, Newcastle," Zoe said brightly, indicating the two-thirds-empty pint glass in front of her.

"Ditto," Chrissy said.

"Stella," Fred chimed in.

Simon leaned forward. "And you, dear?"

Abby flushed. "I think I'm good." She glanced at her own pint glass, perched on the side table to her left. It was completely empty, foam clinging to the inner rim.

Simon arched an eyebrow. "Are you sure?"

"Yes," Abby said. Her head was already buzzing.

"Oh, please." Zoe nudged Abby with her elbow. "Live a little, girl."

"Peer pressure is *not* cool, Zoe," Chrissy said, giggling from her own corner. Her soft Southern accent made Abby smile.

The five had stolen to the West End in search of an authentic British pub. A half hour of searching had yielded the realization that the West End, also the theater and restaurant district, was way too much of a tourist trap to offer anything in the way of authenticity. To Abby, the fevered neon jungle of Leicester Square was comforting in that it reminded her of Times Square—but unfortunately, most of the patrons of the area businesses were, of course, tourists themselves. After oogling the overwhelming colors and flashing electric signage, the group had decided that the best course of action was to make do, and they quickly ducked into one of the seemingly endless "Wolf & Lambs" that they'd passed earlier.

Glancing around the pub again, though, Abby realized that even its cheesy prefab replication of "English" atmosphere was vaguely thrilling. She could tell the others were vibing on the pub, too. They had collapsed into a set of chairs and one sofa propped around a sturdy, aged wooden table next to a big stone fireplace. It was a heavy-handed touch but probably welcome during the bitter winter months. The pub was worn—or carefully arranged to appear as such— and leather-bound books lined the walls. Beer was served at room temperature. A crusty old local telling tales at the

bar would have been the crowning touch, but as it was, the Midwestern couple bickering over the "warm booze" was proof enough that they were, indeed, abroad. A cozy feeling settled over Abby and she grinned lazily. She felt comfortable here.

Either that, or she was drunk.

"I would like another beer," she said, thinking, *What the hell?* again.

"Westminster Abby!" Zoe squealed, slapping her hard on the shoulder. "You go, girl."

"Right. Fred, you'll have to help me carry," Simon said. He and Fred disappeared toward the bar.

Abby leaned back into the sofa again. "Peer pressure is *not* cool," she admonished her friend. "But I'll let it go just this once."

"I'm glad," Zoe replied. "Chrissy is glad. Fred is glad. And Simon is very, very glad."

Chrissy giggled again, more loudly this time, and flipped her honey-colored hair from her face.

"What does *that* mean?" Abby asked.

"Clearly, Simon is crushing on you, big-time," Zoe said.

"No way," Abby protested, eyes wide. She paused. "What makes you think so?"

Zoe chuckled. "Babe, he's been checking you out since we boarded the tube this morning. Do you have no guy radar whatsoever? Not to mention, I am ninety percent sure that the whole reason that he even arranged this outing was to get a chance to talk to you. Which is fine by me. I am happy to pimp out my friends if it means there's a boy with a cute accent buying me drinks."

"Hear, hear," Chrissy said.

"Okay, but... I mean..." Abby started. "Why?"

"Gee, I wonder." Zoe tugged at Abby's ponytail. "I'm sure he finds you hideously unattractive."

Abby blushed. Hideously unattractive, no. She was a bit shy, but she wasn't seriously deficient in the self-confidence department or anything. No, she was fine looking. But when Abby stood next to someone like Dani—as was usually the case with Abby—being quiet generally had the same effect as being invisible.

"What, you don't usually get picked up on?" Zoe asked.

Abby shrugged. "I guess, sometimes."

"But you've got someone back home," Chrissy guessed. "Some cutie."

Abby's blush deepened as she thought of James. James, with whom she had not been in contact in over a month. "No," she said shortly. "Not anymore."

Zoe eyed her cautiously. "Care to talk about it?"

Abby thought for a moment. "It didn't work out," she said simply.

There was an awkward pause, then a new pint glass crashed to the table in front of Abby, beer sloshing over the rim and trailing down the sides of the glass, and the moment was broken.

"Love that full service." Zoe picked up her own beer and took a long, slow pull.

"Enjoy it, because I think it's going to have to be the last round," Fred said. Abby loved his accent, the way his consonants danced against the roof of his mouth. She decided that she was going to have to ask him to teach her to speak Portuguese. At least, like *hello* or *what's up?* She also loved his thick, curly brown hair (as long as it was pulled back into a ponytail) and his deep brown eyes.

"Why?" Zoe asked. She clearly did not love the idea of last call.

Simon tapped the face of his watch. "Dinner. We're expected, front and center, in twenty minutes."

"Oh, crap," Zoe said, taking a healthy swig of her beer. "I hate to be rushed."

"Is the theater fancy in London?" Chrissy asked. "What the heck is 'smart dress,' anyway? I had *no idea* what to wear."

"I just picked the first thing I found at the top of my suitcase," Zoe said.

"Me, too," Abby admitted. "I was way too tired to unpack last night."

"'Smart,' is like, you know sharp, but not necessarily trendy. Pulled together," Simon said.

Simon's accent was thick and heavy. He sounded to Abby like the Lucky Charms leprechaun. A sexy leprechaun. His hair was dark and unkempt and his eyes sparkled emerald. Unfortunately, she could only make out every third word he uttered. Surely this was unfair. Surely she couldn't be expected to adapt to more than one new accent a semester? She leaned forward to better hear what he was saying and she was suddenly eye-to-smiling-Irish-green-eye with Simon. She could practically kiss him, if she wanted to. Just lean right over and plant one on him.

If she wanted to, that is.

"Sharp. Got it," she said.

Simon put his hand on her knee. "You *have* got it, Abby. To be sure, these jeans are brilliant."

"My Levi's?" she stammered. "They're, um, totally old."

"They look perfect." Simon held her gaze for a moment.

"Are we drinking, people? *Tick-tock*," Zoe cut in.

"So we're all going with a loose interpretation of 'smart.' Check," Abby said, sipping daintily.

"Interpret it however you want, dear," Simon said, his freckles skipping across his nose as he beamed at her. "I think you look just lovely."

From: Danishoe@email.com
To: acapshaw1@email.com
Subject: greetings and salutations

Well, hello to my little Union Jack (Or Jackie, whatever, you get the point. I'm *trying* to be cute, here, *chica*. Work with me.)

Just a quick note to see what's the what over in crumpet-ville. Have you seen Hugh Grant yet? Tell him I love him and give him a big, wet kiss for me, willya?

Things are as per usual here in NYC. Summer school started yesterday and I am pleased to report that Elena Basking is sporting a tragic new haircut of the Farrah variety. It's really something to see. I will try to snap a shot on my phone one of these days and shoot you a jpeg because words just can't do justice to the multilayered splendor.

On the male front, Devon Smith did finally get up the courage to call me. Last night, to be specific. Mind you, he *still* hasn't asked me out in so many words, but anyway. Baby steps.

And speaking of boys . . . no, I haven't heard anything from or about James. I know I promised to keep you updated and I swear I absolutely will report any and every detail, but I haven't seen him around. Spencer hasn't mentioned him either. I think he feels guilty for having introduced *el jerko* into your life and giving him the green light and all. I told him there was no need for the self-flagellation, but you know Spence. All protective and whatnot. Big with the hand-wringing. Anyway, you know I'm working for you, but I don't want to put him in any weird, awkward position with his friend. You understand, right?

Besides, what do you care about stupid-face for, anyway? I'm sure you've already charmed the pants off some
unsuspecting native with the whole naive ex-pat thing
you've got going on. Are you wearing the pigtails? Are
you? Are you? Always a hit, those pigtails.

Okay, I should run. Mom wants us to have dinner "as a
family." I keep reminding her that it doesn't count if
Spencer isn't around, but somehow that only makes her
more determined. Go figure. Have fun, and don't do anything I wouldn't do (that should give you plenty of leeway,
right?)!

xoxo,

D

From: acapshaw1@email.com
To: mara16@email.com
Subject: London calling!

Or, rather e-mailing, to be precise.

This place is fantastic. Anything you've seen or read about
England in a movie is pretty much accurate, if exaggerated
(with the exception of Hugh Grant wandering through the
streets looking foppish and disarming, that is), though I
would point out that it's nearly impossible to comprehend
even a word out of anyone's mouth. No joke. The accent
thing is really tripping me up. How's it going with the Italian?

I can't imagine having enough time to see everything that I want to see while I'm here, much less to travel outside of the cities or even—dare I dream—to other countries. Last night we went to dinner and a show with all of the students in the program; the schedule said "smart dress," but since everyone had different ideas about what that meant, it didn't seem to mean anything other than "jeans" and/or "showered."

The dorm is great though it wouldn't *kill* them to install some central air. We each get a single, which is sort of a relief. There are only so many new experiences a girl can take at once, after all.

The kids here are cool. I guess it's what you'd call an international school, heavy on the exchange programs (duh), so there are lots of people here from other countries. I've been hanging with this guy Simon from Ireland and Fred from Portugal. And also a girl named Chrissy from Georgia, which I guess is less exotic, but it's still a far cry from New York City.

My closest friend here so far is a girl named Zoe. She's from Philly. She's pretty punk rock. I mean, she has green streaks in her hair, a pierced tongue, and wears lots of thermals and about six T-shirts at a time—even in the heat! It's really cool. You know we have that skate clique at Hamilton, but that's just not our crowd. I never thought I would be friends with a green-haired comic-book geek (her words, not mine), but we get along really well.

Anyway, classes start tomorrow, so there's a *slight* chance that I will have to buckle down. A little bit.

We'll see.

Write soon and let me know how things are going with you in Florence! Have you met any locals or are you mostly sticking with your fellow S.A.S.S.-ians?

—ttyl,

Abby

From: jameswalker03@email.com

To: acapshaw1@email.com

Subject: how are you?

Dear Abby:

I've now officially sent you six e-mails in the last six weeks, and called you four times. I haven't heard back from you once (but then, you knew that). I'm starting to think you're not interested in talking to me . . .

Seriously, Abby, I get that you're furious. But it was a mistake. It will never happen again and I will make it up to you, I promise.

That is, if you'll let me.

Please don't shut me out, Abby. I miss you.

Love,

James

From: acapshaw1@email.com

To: jameswalker03@email.com

Subject: hello

Hey there—

Just wanted to drop you a quick line to let you know that I arrived in London safe and sound. London is awesome; my list of things to do includes high tea, a double-decker bus tour, and of course, I'm dying to try to get the guards at Buckingham Palace to break character. Oh, and at some point I think I am going to have to try fish and chips.

But enough about me. How's your summer

[delete]

From: acapshaw1@email.com

To: jameswalker03@email.com

Subject: hello

Dear James—

Hi, stranger.

Is it weird to be writing you after a month of no contact? Or is it the month of no contact that's weird? I can't even tell anymore. All I know is that I think I deserve some

[delete]

Westminster Abby

From: acapshaw1@email.com

To: jameswalker03@email.com

Subject: hello

James—

You suck.

[delete]

Chapter Four

"Though British cinema lags behind Hollywood in terms of revenue, recent critical acclaim for a handful of 'art house' pictures have given a credibility to the industry that it once lacked."

Abby squinted at the projection screen propped up behind her professor's head, some thirty rows down from where she sat in the cavernous lecture hall. On it she saw an Indian couple locked in a tight clinch, multicolored flowers glittering vibrantly in the background. British culture was heavily influenced by its Indian population and, according to this lecture, so were some of its better-known movies.

Her own experience of British film was limited to the movie *Bend It Like Beckham*, which she'd seen at an art-house theater in Manhattan one weekend when the latest Reese Witherspoon was sold out. This class was nothing like those she'd taken at Hamilton. Since her British courses fell outside of the domain of her high-school requirements, she'd flipped through the City catalog and registered for anything that sounded interesting. As such, she was taking Social Policy in Post-Industrial England, Intro to Psychology, Shakespearean Conventions in Playwriting, and finally, British Cinema.

Abby glanced at Zoe, who was dressed up for the first day of classes in her S.A.S.S. baby T-shirt (which she'd doctored with a permanent marker to read "*Kick A.S.S.*"), a denim skirt, rainbow-striped kneesocks, and thick-soled mary janes. Zoe looked adorable, but she also looked very bored with the lecture. Aside from Zoe and Abby, the lecture hall was pretty sparsely populated. Abby looked down at her notebook, which glared back up at her, starkly blank. She picked up her pencil and scrawled the words *niche productions* across the top of the page and sat back, considering. She leaned forward again. *Indian culture.* There. That was something.

"There was, in the mid- to late-nineties, an attempt to

mirror the stylistic conventions of such directors as Quentin Tarantino. However, communications monitors frowned on the increasingly violent content of these efforts," the professor continued drily.

"Leave that to the Americans!" someone yelled from the front row. A soft chorus of tittering broke out across the room. Zoe merely rolled her eyes, but Abby flushed, feeling embarrassed and a little bit defensive. Based on the posters, magazines, and billboards she'd seen around campus, the British didn't mind American media all that much. In fact, they were dying to keep up with it. Not to mention, how had they gone from the turn of the century to Quentin Tarantino in the three minutes since she'd last been paying attention? She leafed through the packet of handouts they'd been given at the start of the lecture and consulted the syllabus. *Week 1: Introduction—an overview of the development of British cinema.* Okay, then. That made sense.

She scanned the syllabus. The class would have one midterm in the form of a research paper, and then one final that would be an essay test. That was it. No extra credit, no homework, no nothing. And unlike her high-school classes, where she was assigned specific chapters to read each week that corresponded to the in-class material, here, the last page of her syllabus contained a prodigious list of "suggested reading." What did that mean?

There was no way that she'd be able to make her way through half of these books, not even if she started this afternoon and didn't come out of her dorm again until August. Apparently British students were trusted to read what was appropriate until they felt adequately self-educated on the relevant subject matter. She looked over at Zoe, who had slid far enough down in her seat to prop up her feet on the back of the chair in front of her. Abby sincerely doubted Zoe's motivation regarding the suggested reading list.

The Indian-themed slide had given way to a scene from *Pulp Fiction*, and from there to a varied montage of Helena Bonham Carter tripping her way through a selection of Merchant-Ivory features. The room was dark, and very warm. It was all Abby could do to stay awake. And based on the hush that had fallen over the room since the Tarantino joke, she wasn't the only one. Zoe had slid a pair of sunglasses down her face, and Abby had a sneaking suspicion that behind the darkened lenses her friend's eyes were closed. Abby wasn't usually this susceptible to sleeping in class. But now she was in England, and there was a first time for anything.

"Hi, honey, how was the rest of your day?" Zoe asked, sliding her cafeteria tray down onto the table and settling in next to Abby.

"Fine," Abby said. She regarded her tray with a lack of

enthusiasm. "Until now, I guess. Lunch leaves something to be desired."

Zoe smiled and bit into a french fry. "Blech. Dry. I asked the woman behind the counter for ketchup and she looked at me like I had three heads."

Abby laughed. "Try the vinegar," she said, sliding a bottle of it over. "It's not the same, but it's not bad."

Zoe shrugged. "Vinegar, huh? I guess I may as well. If you can't beat 'em, join 'em." She grabbed the bottle and shook it vigorously over her plate. "I'm a little bit worried that I'm now eating french fries three times a day. Oh, excuse me, *chips.*" She peered at Abby's plate. "What the hell are *you* eating?"

"It's a baked potato with tuna," Abby said, trying to sound more enthusiastic than she felt. "I like tuna. I like potatoes. How bad can it be?"

"You tell me," Zoe said. "I notice you haven't exactly wolfed it down."

Abby reached for her fork and speared a big bite. She chewed for a moment, contemplating, and then put her fork back down on her plate. She pushed her chair back quickly, rising to her feet.

"Where are you going?" Zoe called out, trying in vain to suppress her laughter.

"I think I'm going to grab some chips," Abby said.

"Get some extra vinegar while you're at it!"

• • •

From: capshawclan@email.com
To: acapshaw1@email.com
Subject: fun news!

Hi sweetie—

Daddy and I were pleased to hear from you (better late than never!), and are glad to know that you are settling in and having a good time. It sounds like you are making friends as well. We'd love to meet Zoe sometime when you're both back Stateside.

Your class schedule certainly sounds interesting; I had no idea that touring could be considered part of the curriculum! But you're probably right to make use of the course offerings since this might be your only chance to study Shakespeare in his hometown. It's a good thing that you each have singles; it will make it easier for you in terms of studying and even sleeping not to have to worry about being disturbed by someone else. Reuben assures me that this system works very well for the students under his charge.

I notice you didn't mention the library. Have you checked on its hours yet? According to the online map of the campus, it's just down the block from you. Let me know what you think of it once you've had a chance to swing by.

Well, I should go. Your father will be home soon and we'll need to have dinner.

Love,

Mom

After she'd read her mother's e-mail, Abby returned to her room. She was feeling disheartened. It wasn't any surprise that her mom had already had *multiple* conversations with Reuben about City College, or that she knew down to the very campus address where the library was located. In fact, Abby was even a little surprised that her mom hadn't included the library hours in her e-mail. Abby should have been frustrated. Or maybe even furious. After all, she was miles away and her parents were still trying to control her! But really, she felt slightly homesick. How could she be homesick for a place where she felt so suffocated?

She flopped backward on her bed, awash in self-pity. She thought of putting on her most depressing music but standing up again would require too much energy. Mostly she thought she'd mope for a little while and then maybe head down to the lounge for a quick chocolate fix.

A loud rap on the door startled her from her thoughts. She opened it to find Zoe standing in her doorway looking impatient. "Excuse me, but you said you were just quickly going to check your e-mail. What happened? Why didn't you come down to the hall bar to find me? And why do you look all depression queen-y?" she asked, tapping at the face of her Astro Boy watch.

"I am in a horrible mood. Unfit for the public," Abby explained.

"Please. I am *always* unfit for the public. That's what

makes me fun. Now, is this what you're wearing?"

Abby glanced down at her outfit. She was wearing her perennial jeans, flip-flops, and a tiny cotton cardigan over a tank top. The summers in London, she was learning, weren't all that warm. "Clearly. Why?"

Zoe waved her hand impatiently. "Whatever, it's fine. We're only going to the hall bar, after all."

Before Abby could even protest, Zoe grabbed her hand and dragged her through the doorway.

The advantage of the hall bar was that it was literally right in their lobby.

It was already packed when Abby and Zoe arrived. "God, it's crowded," Abby said.

"Yeah, it was dead when we first got here, but then, you know, it started filling up."

They maneuvered their way to the front of the crowd and ordered two pints. "Guinness," she mouthed to Abby. "A man's drink."

"Is that a good thing?" Abby asked.

"Trust me," Zoe said.

Once the beers were ready, the girls sidled up to a corner of the bar, establishing a space for themselves. Abby took a sip of her beer and nearly choked.

"Yeah, it's very thick," Zoe said sympathetically. "I should have warned you."

Abby pushed the drink aside. "Maybe it's an acquired taste."

"Maybe. In which case, you'll have plenty of chances to acquire it now that we're in London."

"So who were you here with earlier?" Abby looked around for people she knew, but the patrons were stacked nearly one on top of another, making it an impossible task.

"The usual suspects. Simon, Fred, Chrissy. Chrissy had a friend from class with her, some chick named Melanie." The look on Zoe's face suggested that she'd been none too impressed with Melanie.

"What was wrong with her?" Abby asked.

"Nothing, really," Zoe explained. "She was just boring. *Simon* seemed to like her, though."

"What?" Abby asked. She grabbed at Zoe's forearm. "Are you holding out gossip on me?"

Zoe grinned sheepishly. "I think they left together a little while ago."

Abby clapped her hand over her mouth. "Craziness! Go, Simon!" she exclaimed.

Zoe looked at Abby skeptically. "You're not upset?"

"Why would I be upset?" Abby asked.

"Because just the other day he was macking on you, hon, so I thought maybe you would be jealous."

Abby laughed. "Please. No. Honestly, Simon's so sweet—and I love the Irish brogue—but...well, I'm not really looking to get into things right now. Romance things, you know."

Zoe raised an eyebrow. "Because..." she prompted.

"Well..." Abby hedged. Even *she* had grown a little bit tired of the story by now. But then again, Zoe wasn't the type of person to ask a question if she didn't really want to know the answer. "Okay, you want to know the truth? About why I'm in London?"

"Always," Zoe said, rubbing her hands together with glee. "This sounds good."

Abby sighed. "The thing is, my parents are really controlling. *Really* controlling."

"*How* controlling?" Zoe asked.

"Let's put it this way: I'm never allowed to go out on weekends unless it's to my friend Dani's house, and even then they usually call to check in on me."

"Wow," Zoe said. "That sucks."

"I know!" Abby agreed. "The thing is, I've always been a really good student and really well behaved; like, I've never given them any reason to be so overprotective.

"Anyway, this year, I decided I was going to try to be a little bit different, you know—do things that were exciting and stuff. And so one night my friend Dani and I went to a party at a bar and I met this guy. James."

"It always comes back to a guy." Zoe shook her head. "When will we chicks learn?"

"He was really cute, a freshman in college. And into funky music and stuff, like punk rock and electronica. He used to make me playlists. Anyway, we started dating without my parents knowing."

"Let me guess: They found out and went ballistic?" Zoe asked.

Abby nodded. "You have no idea. They said I was too young to date. That I couldn't date before I was seventeen."

Zoe gasped melodramatically, splaying one hand out across her chest. "No!"

"Yes. And then I introduced them to James. But that just made things worse. They thought he was no good because he was 'artsy' and an English major. You know, not pre-med or whatever. I was trying to work the 'college-man maturity' angle, but apparently English isn't 'practical' enough, so that backfired. They wanted to know why a college guy would be dating a high-school girl, anyway. And they told me that I couldn't see him anymore."

"But you still did?"

Abby looked away. "I was in love with him. Or at least I thought I was. What was I supposed to do?"

"So that's a yes, then."

"Yeah, I still saw him. And I lied to them about it. Which was totally unlike me. But they figured it out. And then they decided that if I couldn't break up with him myself, they'd do it for me. So they found this program and signed me up. Which, under any other circumstances, would have been totally amazing. But of course I was furious. But *way* too much of a goody-goody to sabotage the application."

"So where's James now? At home, pining away?"

Abby shook her head vehemently. "Not even. Here's the really funny part. I cried for about a week, and argued with my parents bitterly, but ultimately, I had to apply. I mean, I really didn't have a choice. After all of the applications were in, and I was set to go, I used up all of my savings and bought him a plane ticket to London so that he could visit me midsummer. Then—" she broke off abruptly, her throat thick.

"Then, what?" Zoe asked softly.

"I found out that he was cheating on me." Even now, the words cut. Abby's eyes welled up with tears.

"He cheated on you?" Zoe repeated, incredulous.

"Oh, no," Abby said. "It wasn't that he had *cheated*, once. He *was cheating*, for as long as I had known him."

"What a jerk," Zoe said. "Guys are such losers."

"I know," Abby agreed. "I couldn't believe it. I was totally thrown. Suddenly, though, I was really glad to be going to London for the semester. To get away and try something new and exciting. On my own." She managed a small smile. "James doesn't have to be my 'exciting thing.' He probably shouldn't be, when you think about it."

"Damn straight!" Zoe said.

"So what about you?" Abby asked, changing the subject. "What are you doing here?"

"Are you kidding? London, England? The birthplace of Sid and Nancy, the Sex Pistols, and punk rock? The home of the Tate Modern and Camden Market? I've been dying to come here all my life!"

"And your parents were cool with it?" Abby asked.

"Totally. They're really open. I mean, look at the way that I dress," Zoe replied, pointing one black-tipped fingernail at a huge hole in her carpenter jeans. "They don't care."

Abby sighed. She couldn't imagine what it would be like to have parents like that. "It must be nice," she said.

"Yeah, the only people who were really upset about my leaving were my band members," Zoe said. "But they got over it when I promised to bring them back clothing from the flea markets."

"You're in a band?" Abby asked, laughing. "Why does that not surprise me? What do you play?"

"Drums." Zoe broke out into an impromptu rhythm on her pint glass. Abby shimmied in time for a moment.

"That's quite a show you two've got going on. You should take your act on the town."

Abby and Zoe looked up to find themselves being observed by a boy. A very attractive boy, to be precise. He was tall and well built, solid in a striped T-shirt that outlined the muscles of his chest. He wore close-fitting jeans that emphasized his long legs, and sneakers—all of which Abby was beginning to realize was the style: halfway between "trendy" and "casual." It really suited him.

"You wanna dance, cowboy?" Zoe drawled, in an exaggerated Southern accent.

"Not just now, thank you. I've got a round of cards to lose with my mates over there." He gestured with his pint glass, and then turned to Abby. "But maybe you can join us in a bit, persuade me to change my mind. Or at the very least, turn my luck around. I'm crap at poker, it would seem." His bright green eyes twinkled.

"Oh, uh—" Abby stammered.

"Right. Presumptuous of me. A stranger and all. And maybe you're crap at poker, too." He held out his free hand to shake. "I'm Ian."

"I'm Abby," she managed. Ian's hand was warm and strong.

"Great. Well, now we're not strangers, are we?" he asked. He ran a hand through his close-cropped, sandy-blond hair, and Abby found herself wondering what it would feel like between her fingers. "So now you've no excuse but to come by."

He marched off, leaving Abby to gape after him.

"Nice one, Abby." Zoe laughed. "Very smooth. Tell me again about how you're not looking to get into things right now? Romance things?"

But Abby was too distracted to answer. She was busy watching Ian.

Who, she noticed, had turned from his table to watch her.

Chapter Five

"Zoe, what are you doing?"

Abby sighed in exasperation as her friend dug into her studded black messenger bag and whipped out a pair of rhinestone-trimmed black plastic cat's-eye glasses. "Since when do you even *wear* glasses? I've been in class with you and I have never seen those!"

Zoe shot Abby a withering look. "I only wear my glasses when there's something to see. Class does *not* count."

"She wants to make sure that she doesn't miss it if Prince William walks by," Simon quipped.

"He's so dreamy." Zoe sighed and pretended to swoon.

"I wouldn't have pegged him for your type," Abby commented. "Kind of, um, preppy. Anyway, seeing as how it's the middle of the summer, I'm sort of doubting that he's here."

"You never know. Maybe he's doing a summer session," Zoe suggested.

"Not according to *Hello*," Melanie offered. She was the group's de facto expert on British tabloid culture. "Also? He's, like, twentysomething. So I don't even think he's still enrolled."

It was the group's first postorientation weekend, and Abby, Zoe, Simon, Melanie, Chrissy, and Fred had taken the tube to Windsor to see Eton, the very chichi private school where Prince William, Harry, and other children of royalty and dignitaries attended. In England, private schools were called public schools, which was extremely confusing to Abby. But the gist was that the place was fancy. Visitors could pay a small fee and tour the chapel, the school yard, the cloisters, and the Museum of Student Life. So far, though, all their group had done was stroll along the edge of the Thames and speculate as to where Prince William was hiding himself.

"I think we should check out the school yard," Abby suggested. "I mean, it's a sunny day—which seems to be a total rare thing. We should take advantage of it."

"I agree," Chrissy chimed in. "Anyway, there are no royals anywhere to be found."

Zoe rolled her eyes. "Fine," she said. She waggled her glasses up and down. "Spoil my fun."

"I think there's a statue of Henry the Sixth in the school yard," Simon offered. "Fancy a picture?" He smiled and winked at Melanie, and waved his digital camera at her.

"Doesn't anyone want to go into Windsor Castle and check out the artwork?" Abby asked. "Rarest in England..." She waved her guidebook tauntingly.

Zoe sighed. "Yes, dear. We will go see the artwork after Simon has taken his precious photo of Melanie in the yard. But only on one condition."

Abby raised an eyebrow questioningly. "Which is?"

"That you give that book a rest for an hour or two, babe."

The next morning on their way to class, Abby and Zoe looked at the City campus with jaded eyes.

"Somehow, I think we got the short end of the stick," Zoe quipped.

Abby glanced in the direction that Zoe was indicating. Unlike the elegant, historic Eton campus, their college was typical postwar, constructed of nondescript concrete. But for Abby, the appeal of City College had much more to do with its participation in the S.A.S.S. exchange program than its architecture.

"Yeah, but it's cool that we're right in the heart of London, don't you think?"

Zoe nodded. "Definitely."

"Oh, good. I'd hate to think you were dissatisfied with our educational offerings here at City," a voice behind them said.

Abby turned and immediately flushed. *Ian.* He was smiling mischievously. She opened her mouth to craft a reply, but was cut off by Zoe before she could get any words out.

"Sorry to dis on your school. Now what's your story? Are you following us?"

It was true that he did seem to be around a lot. Abby had classes only three days a week, but somehow she bumped into Ian almost every day, whether in the library or outside a lecture hall. She'd just assumed it was a coincidence, even though she secretly hoped it sort of wasn't. She waited to see what he would say to Zoe.

"Naturally," he answered. "You know I have a thing for Americans." He winked at Abby.

"Fair enough." Zoe shrugged with a smirk. "How come we haven't seen you in the hall bar lately?"

"I've been playing cards with my mates back at the flat," he explained. "We've got a right competition going."

Zoe nodded. "No girls allowed. I get it."

"Well..." Ian smiled again, this time staring straight at Abby. "It is sort of a boys' club. I think it would feel a bit laddish for you lot if you were to stop by. But maybe I can make time for the hall bar one of these evenings."

"We'll be there," Zoe promised.

"Will *you*?" Ian repeated, still holding Abby's gaze.

Abby blushed even deeper. "We will," she assured him, her voice a tinny squeak.

"Perfect," he said, and loped off.

From: acapshaw1@email.com

To: Danishoe@email.com

Subject: London calling!

Attachments: me_and_Harri.jpg

Just wondering how many times I can use "London calling!" before it gets old. What's that you say? It's already old? Yeah, I figured as much.

Anyway, I can't believe it's been almost three weeks since I came to London! I've been hanging with that girl I mentioned, Zoe, pretty much full-time. I never thought she and I would get along as well as we do—I mean, the girl has green hair—but maybe we've got a yin-yang thing going on or something.

We're touring like mad, sometimes through organized outings with our program, and sometimes just on our own. We were at Buckingham Palace last week to see the changing of the guards. I read somewhere that those uniforms weigh like forty pounds or something. That's pretty serious. Of course Zoe rushed the procession to try and get the Beefeaters to laugh (they're not allowed to break their concentration or show any facial expressions). But needless to say their security is pretty tight, and she didn't exactly make it. I'm not sure we're welcome back at the palace anytime soon...

We also caught a street juggler at the Covent Garden piazza. Covent Garden is this fabulous extension of the West End with amazing shopping, all kinds of food vendors (again, chocolate and chips are seriously becoming my main staple), and crazed, funky action on the streets. There's a man dressed like a robot who mimes basically round the clock. Next time we're there I'll take a picture.

Don't worry, though—we're not only about touring, museums, and culture. We've done the supercheese thing, too. We hit Madame Tussaud's, the wax museum (just like the one in Times Square, except this one is the original). Pretty hilarious. So now I have a shot of myself mock-making out with Harrison Ford from *Raiders* (from a distance of three feet; you're not allowed to actually touch the figures). And if you open the attachment to the e-mail, you'll have it, too.

I also should mention that I have been consorting with the locals of late. We've all been hanging in the hall bar almost every night and so we're starting to get friendly with the real, full-time British students who are here for the summer session. Of course I mostly stick to Coke when we're out; if I drank every time we hung out in the hall bar, I would barely be lucid enough to remember my time here!

In particular, I keep running into this guy Ian. I don't actually have any classes with him, but somehow I see him

whenever I'm on the university campus. And lately he is always in the bar when I'm there, usually playing poker with his friends. (And making fun of me because I always refuse to join. But, please. I am not one for gambling.) And, inexplicably, when I was wandering through the Barbican last week (a huge, futuristic arts center that's around the corner from our school), I bumped into him, again. He was all by himself. Turns out he was going to see a movie. Barbican plays American films occasionally (always at least a month behind!). He asked if I wanted to join him, but I made up some excuse. It was too weird—I kind of thought he was just being nice, and you know I'm not great with the spontaneity.

So, he seems cool. Just, you know, in a friendly way. I mean, I'm sure the invitation was friendly.

Mostly sure.

And like I told you a hundred times, I'm hardly looking for anything right now. I need some time on my own, to get over the James situation.

Right?

From: Danishoe@email.com
To: acapshaw1@email.com
Subject: Re: London calling!

Yeah, you've got it bad, girl.

Chapter Six

"Okay, now, *how* did you know about this place, Zoe? 'Cause I am a hundred and twenty percent sure that you don't have a guidebook of your own!"

"Oh, Abby." Zoe sighed playfully. "Simple, naive Abby."

"This place" was Camden Town, an enclave in North London dedicated to lurid, tawdry, alternative consumerism. Abby had read that it was one of the few sections of the city that had successfully warded off gentrification, and judging from the chaos before her, it was the truth. Other than the day she had spent at the London Zoo, she had never seen such an eclectic group of people in

one space. She credited the variety to the wealth of goods available in the outdoor market, an oversize flea market brimming with everything from posters, to used books, to mix CDs, to clothing. Already Zoe had bought herself a leather bracelet and a long-sleeve T-shirt with the tube symbol on it ("I absolutely *cannot* wear this until I am back in Philly," she had told Abby with a grimace, "but what the hell?"), and Abby had been seriously swayed by a pair of knockoff designer sunglasses that were way out of her price range.

"Look, babe, it's like I told you," Zoe continued, "the minute I got into punk rock and modern art, I was gone. I knew I had to come to London. To tell you the truth, I'll probably come back for college," she said, "if I can find an art program that I like.

"Are you ever going to buy that?" she asked, pointing at a bracelet Abby had been fingering for the better part of ten minutes. "I'm starting to get claustrophobic."

The alleys in between the individual booths teemed with people, each weaving his or her way through the aisles at different paces.

"Ten quid," said the razor-thin, multitattooed lady manning the jewelry booth.

Abby wrinkled her nose. "That's a lot," she whispered to Zoe.

"Abbs! What do I keep saying? You are going to have to learn how to live a little while you're here!"

"Is there a way to 'live a little' that doesn't involve spending thirty bucks on a plastic bracelet? I mean, it's cute, but I could make one like this myself, at home," Abby protested.

"Ah yes, the pragmatic argument. Fine. You don't want to spend money? I get it. But there are other ways to have fun here!"

"Such as?" Abby asked.

Zoe dragged Abby through the crush toward a man selling, of all things, boots. High, platform-heeled, psychedelic boots in busy patterns and blinding hues. Abby had never tried on shoes outside of an actual shoe store. The situation seemed a little bit fishy to her.

"Here." Zoe reached up and snatched a pair. "These. You're going to try these on for me."

Abby's eyebrows flew upward. "Not. In. A. Million. Years."

The boots were zebra-printed and thigh-high, and sat on four-inch platforms. They laced up the sides. The soles of the shoes were a neon shade of pink.

The boots were, in Abby's opinion, completely out of the question.

"I'll give you that they're more me than you," Zoe admitted. "But I don't care. I'm not asking you to wear them on your college interviews. Just to try them on and then have a look at yourself in the mirror. Trust me—take a walk on the wild side!"

"They're not my size," Abby pointed out.

"What size are you?" Zoe asked.

"Seven."

Before Zoe could say anything else, the small, wiry man in the booth disappeared into a mountain of shoeboxes. After a moment and some rustling, he emerged with an oversize box, triumphant. Zoe grinned and handed the box to Abby.

"I do *not* see how these are going to fit over my jeans."

"Be creative, hon," Zoe said. "I have faith in you."

After several minutes of tugging, grunting, and yanking, Abby managed to slide the boots up and over her jeans.

"Now," Zoe said, taking her by the shoulders and positioning her in front of the full-length mirror propped up toward the back of the booth. "*Please* check yourself out."

Abby gazed at her reflection in disbelief. Her alter ego was impossibly tall and, due to the tilt of the mirror, thin and angular, all legs. Her jeans stretched practically to her chin. Her hair was pulled into a casual but cute bun at the top of her head, and thanks to a makeup counter they'd hit about an hour ago, she was freshly glossed and glowing. Somehow, in this context, the boots didn't look so outrageous. In fact, they looked kind of... sexy. A slow smile spread across Abby's face. No, it wasn't a college-interview outfit, but then, she wasn't on a college interview, was she? For now, at least, she could get used to this look.

"Yeah, girl, you look hot!" Zoe laughed. "And you know it, too!"

"What can I say?" Abby replied. "It's hard work being this cute." She struck a fashion-model pose, deliberately exaggerating the thrust of her hips and the pout of her lips.

"Work it!" Zoe shrieked, clapping wildly.

Abby sashayed back and forth down the small clearing adjacent to the booth. Zoe forced impressively realistic beat-box noises from the back of her throat, keeping time.

"Fabulous, darling, that's perfect. Just hold it right there, sweetie," a voice from beside her said.

Abby froze, nearly falling over backward in her sky-scraper heels. She recovered at the last moment, wobbling back and forth slightly. She recognized that voice. She looked up, not daring to breathe.

Ian stood at the entryway to the booth. His right hand was hooked casually into the front pocket of his baggy cords, and he was smirking. "Brilliant," he said, mime-snapping a photograph. "We'll make a star of you yet."

"What are you doing here?" Abby asked.

"Shopping," he said, as though the answer should be obvious to anyone. Which, Abby realized, it should. There weren't many other things to do in Camden Market. "There's a new record that's come out from Rob's—my flatmate's—favorite DJ, a remix, and I promised to meet him here to buy it."

"Well," Abby said. "Oh." Her arms, dangling uselessly at her sides, suddenly felt twelve times too long. She self-consciously crossed them in front of her chest.

"You going to be at the hall bar tonight?" Ian asked suddenly.

"I . . . don't know," Abby stammered.

"Of course," Zoe cut in. "Though Abby might be over-dressed for the occasion."

"Right, the boots." Ian chuckled. "They're dead trendy, Abby. But she's right, you might feel a bit out of place at the hall bar. It's meant to be more of a casual vibe, just for mucking around with the lads."

"And birds," Zoe added helpfully, adopting her accent straight out of *My Fair Lady*.

"Anyway," Ian continued, still pretending, to his credit, that this conversation was not, in fact, happening in some far-flung alternate reality but was actually completely smooth, normal, and nonsocially awkward, "you ought to come round. I could teach you a thing or two about card games, you know."

Any semblance of an appropriate response flew from Abby's head. It didn't matter, though. Ian had already turned to leave. "I'm late to meet Rob." He glanced at his watch. "But hopefully I'll see you tonight. Cheers." Then he paused, giving Abby another slow once-over. "I take back what I said about being overdressed. You can wear those if you like. They suit you."

He was gone before Abby could think to say thank you.

Once he was out of earshot, Zoe let out a low whistle. "Well, dear, I hope you're not thinking of skipping the bar tonight. Even if you don't buy the boots, you definitely had better make an appearance."

Abby flushed. "Um, I guess I can," she said.

"You guess?" Zoe winked knowingly. She grabbed her friend's hand. "Let's at least get you a fun lip gloss for this evening."

In the end, Abby decided that understated was the way to go. After a brief struggle with the animal-print thigh-highs, she managed to slither out of the boots and part ways with them, but Zoe did eventually talk her into replacing her rather simple, conservative black leather wallet with a huge plastic affair studded with rainbow sequins that they had found at a different booth. "Superfun," Zoe had proclaimed, prompting Abby to declare the phrase her new mantra.

Now, back in the hall bar, Abby unzipped her nifty new superfun wallet and counted out two pounds in coinage. After three-plus weeks abroad, it still bothered her that the single pounds were coins rather than bills, making it all too easy to forget that the tiny round pieces were worth almost twice a dollar. She slid them across the bar and ordered a Coke. England was a pub culture, but the point was to relax with your friends and socialize, not to get drunk, thankfully.

Abby was preoccupied, anyway. The last thing she needed was a drink stronger than a soda. After running into Ian in Camden Market, Zoe had insisted that they go to the hall bar that night. Of course, to be honest, Abby hadn't needed too much convincing. Why shouldn't she take Ian up on his offer to get to know him a little better? He was cute, and funny, and near as she could tell, genuinely interested in her. And as she had told Dani, she'd technically been broken up with James for a while now. Maybe she *was* ready to date again. Maybe she wasn't—but there was no way to find out without hitting the hall bar to see if Ian was around.

Which was what she was doing now, all the while trying desperately to appear casual, leaning against the bar, sipping at her soda, scanning the room. True, she had done her hair in the pigtails again—sort of the fashion equivalent of knocking on wood—but nobody here knew that.

Zoe was in the corner talking to Melanie and Simon, who, since they'd met, had become as inseparable as Siamese twins. Fred, Abby knew, was in his room resting. He and Chrissy planned to go clubbing later. He'd invited Abby and Zoe, but Zoe wouldn't let Abby off of the hook about meeting Ian, and besides, without the scary boots she'd tried at the market, Abby really didn't have anything to wear. She knew she would have to go clubbing at least once before she left—the UK DJ scene being widely known as preeminent—but for now, the disco wallet was as superfun as she was going to get.

There. Abby's breath caught in her throat. At the front door, wearing a cotton polo with the collar turned up slightly and dark jeans. It was Ian, flanked on either side by a friend, looking happy and freshly showered. No, it was more than that, Abby realized, seeing his hair carefully tousled and guessing that there was some slightly manic styling action going on in there. He looked more than showered. He looked *primped.* Had he primped for her? She resisted the urge to bolt for the bathroom to slather on a fresh layer of her new lip gloss.

Then there was the problem of actually talking to him. She could play coy, and march directly over to Zoe and company without even a glance in Ian's direction. Or she could be light about it, brushing past him deliberately with a well-timed *hi* before setting up shop with her friends. And there was always the mature route, she realized, of simply walking up to him and saying hello, pretenses be damned.

No, she might have a superfun, splashy new wallet, and flirty pigtails, but that was about as outgoing as it got for her. She was getting set to gather up her soda and weave her way over to Zoe when she felt a tap on her shoulder.

"Playing hard to get, are we?"

She looked up to see Ian standing beside her, his green eyes twinkling.

"I—what—no." Abby suppressed a cough and forced another sip of soda down her throat.

"Can't fool me; I saw you calculating the distance between the bar and your mates, trying to figure out the best route over there without having to cross paths with me," he teased. "Too bad I'm on to you." He tugged at the tip of one of her ponytails. "Very Spice Girls."

"Well . . ." Abby said. She shifted her weight, desperately searching the depths of her brain for a follow-up question. "So, uh, what year are you?"

"First," he said. "So only a year or two older than yourself."

"I didn't mean—" Abby started. Why was it that everything Ian said managed to get under her skin and render her nearly speechless? She was shy but she wasn't socially *challenged* by any means. And yet. "So you're studying . . ."

"Economics," he said. Abby knew that British teens had to apply to specific courses when they went off to university; unlike American students, who had the luxury of waiting until sophomore or junior year of college before declaring a major, the English needed to decide what they wanted to study quite early on.

"Cool," she said. Then she smiled. Really, it was sad, how little she had to offer by way of unstilted conversation.

Ian laughed. "Cooool," he replied in an exaggerated American accent.

"And where are you from?" Abby continued, finally finding her conversational footing.

"Manchester," he said. "In the North, about two hours
from here. Very industrial. Very different from London.
Once I've had a few more pints you'll hear the accent
creep out."

"In that case, the next one's on me," Abby said.

"A woman after my own heart."

"So, how come I never see you in the dorms?" Abby
asked. "You're always on campus but never in the dining
hall."

"I'm here at the hall bar all the time these days. Terrible
for my bank account. But I don't live in the dorms. Have a
flat just down the street with Rob and Luke." He gestured
to his friends, who had hunkered down at a corner table
and immediately begun cutting cards.

"So you don't eat in the dining halls?" Given that he
didn't live in Finsbury, it was actually interesting how often
she *did* see him.

"No, we've got a nice-size kitchen and we do quite a bit
of cooking. Rather impressive, actually, for a bunch of
blokes on their own."

"I'll believe it when I see it." She grinned.

"Is that a challenge?" Ian asked, raising an eyebrow.

Abby thought for a moment. *Was* it? If it was, then she
was effectively asking him to cook for her—in other words,
suggesting a dinner date. That went well beyond the

boundaries of even superfun Abby, hot-fudge-sundae Abby, or any permutation that extended beyond the reaches of her imagination. Asking Ian out was a statement, an active decision.

One she was ready to make.

"As a matter of fact, it is." She replaced her drink on the bar and extended her hand, daring Ian to shake on the deal.

"Accepted," he said, grasping her hand without hesitation. "With pleasure!"

"You'll be sorry," Abby said, still smiling.

"Unlikely," Ian said. "Tomorrow night, my flat. Just down the street, on Beech. Number 242, flat 3B."

"I don't have a pen. I'll never remember this."

Ian conferred quickly with the bartender, who did indeed have a pen. He scrawled the information on a cocktail napkin and passed it to Abby. "What time do you normally get hungry?" he asked.

"Whenever." Abby shrugged. She could always eat.

"Well, I normally get hungry around half-seven," he decided. "Does that work for you?"

"Sure," Abby said. "If you are absolutely positive that you don't mind cooking for me."

Ian trained his electric-green eyes on Abby. The look he gave her left no room for doubt. "Abby, dear, you don't even know."

She looked at him quizzically.

"I love a challenge," he said.

Chapter Seven

From: acapshaw1@email.com

To: Danishoe@email.com

Subject: newsflash on the boy front

Hi there—

Interesting developments going on over on this side of the pond. As in, your little Abby's all growed up! Brace yourself, babe.

Abby asked a boy out! On a date! And he said yes!

No joke. His name is Ian, you know, the British guy I

mentioned before? He's totally, totally adorable. Sort of what you think of when you imagine boys from London. Or, at least, what *I* thought of when I imagined London boys. Tall and thin, but with some build to him, always dressed somewhere between casual and trendy, which is basically the norm for the city. Various pairs of Pumas and lots of layered T-shirts. Bright green eyes, dark blond hair. Hairstyle straight out of *Teen People*'s "Twenty-one Under 21" list (think: pomade). Messenger bags. You see where I'm going.

Remember, I told you I kept bumping into him and it didn't exactly seem like he minded? So, finally, we got to talking, and he mentioned that he liked to cook…and I suggested he cook *for me*! Crazy, right? Looking back, I don't know how I had the guts to do it.

I'm supposed to meet him in—oops!—an hour. Which means I should probably get ready. Zoe has put a moratorium on my black tank tops, so we borrowed one from Chrissy that's bright pink and ribbed. It hits in all the right places, if I do say so myself.

Must run. I still need to shower and I want to pick up some wine beforehand. That's what you do for dinner dates, right?

xoxo,

me

• • •

Abby stood on the doorstep of number 242 Beech, consulting the wrinkled cocktail napkin she'd fished from her pocket. *Apartment 3B.* There it was, written in plain black and white. The building had been easy to find and the individual apartment buzzers were clearly labeled. There was no putting it off any longer.

She was here.

Abby's hands felt clammy and her throat was dry. Her stomach was twisted into thorny knots of anxiety. What had she been *thinking* when she invited herself over to Ian's? Who did things like that? Never mind that he'd seemed pretty pleased at the suggestion. To ask someone to cook for you—that wasn't courageous, it was all-out rude!

Abby knew that her doubts were due more to nerves than anything else. After all, her parents hadn't wanted her to date, and the fact was that until now, she mostly hadn't. Other than James, of course. She was relatively unskilled in the Art of the Flirt. Now she was going to have to flirt—or at the very least talk—to Ian, one-on-one, all night.

If she was lucky.

She racked her brain for possible conversation topics. Favorite movies, music, books. Names of childhood pets. Food allergies. She couldn't come up with one solid example for any category. Her mind was a blank. This wasn't good.

Well, she realized, *I have two choices. I can either flee in terror and spend the night in my pajamas, or I can suck it up and ring the damn buzzer.*

Fleeing sounded appealing, but it wasn't really an option. If she stood Ian up, she'd never be able to set foot in the hall bar again. Fine, then. It was now or never. With a deep breath, she reached out and pressed the buzzer. At the staticky response of the intercom, she pushed the front door open and ventured inside.

She wandered up the stairs until she came to the third floor. Most British buildings referred to their first floor as "ground floor," so she actually had to climb four flights.

Ian's roommate Rob greeted her at the door. "Abby!" he exclaimed, his curly red hair exploding in all directions. He flung his arms around her as if they were old friends as opposed to people who sometimes happened to see each other in the same bar. It was unsettling, but also appealing, Abby decided. "Come on in!"

"I don't think we've ever officially met," she said.

"You're the girl who never wants to play poker." He smiled.

"I'm no good at cards." She shook her head. It was hard to stay nervous when Rob's affable energy was overtaking the atmosphere. She stepped into the common room of the apartment and surveyed the room. "Is Ian here?"

"He's in the kitchen," Rob explained. "I think there's been a bit of trouble."

"That doesn't sound good," Abby said, her brow creasing in concern. "Should I go investigate?"

Rob pointed toward the kitchen and Abby tentatively tiptoed over.

The first thing she noticed about the kitchen was that it was large by New York standards, in that there was space enough to fit a full-size table. The second thing she noticed was an aluminum pan laid upon said table, and on the pan an unidentified blackened mass hissing and smoking ominously.

Ian took the wine from Abby and set it down on the counter. He leaned forward and kissed her on the cheek. "I'm afraid I've some bad news regarding dinner."

Abby gestured toward the pan. "I take it that was dinner?"

Ian nodded sadly. "*Was* being the operative word. That was guinea fowl, actually, and meant to be roasted rather than burned to a crisp, at that."

Abby wasn't completely sure what guinea fowl was, but she also wasn't sure that she minded having something else for dinner, either. "Oh," she said, hoping to sound enthusiastic. "I've never had . . . guinea fowl."

"Right, well, I'm the git. I shouldn't have gone for something so elaborate. I was trying to impress you. Which of course, by now I've lost all hope of."

"No, hey," Abby protested. "I mean, that's amazing, what you did—tried to do. I've never even *heard* of guinea

fowl, to be totally honest. And I've for sure never tried to cook it. So that's something. You get an A for effort."

Ian burst out laughing. "You're very kind," he said. "But it appears I've lost our challenge. Which means that you get to pick the alternative. Restaurant, that is. There are two places nearby that I like, up near the Angel tube. One is sushi and one is seafood. And, of course, there's always curry takeaway."

Abby paused for a moment, considering her options. "How about curry, then? Since everyone keeps telling me I have to try the Indian food in London."

"You haven't yet?" Ian raised his eyebrows in disbelief. "Well, then, it's settled." He opened a drawer in the kitchen and pulled out a menu.

"You're in charge of the order," Abby insisted. "I'm totally in your hands."

Three hours later, takeaway containers emptied and pushed aside, Abby and Ian lay stretched across opposite ends of the couch of his common room. Rob had fled the scene shortly after he'd let Abby in, and Ian had explained that Luke was home with his parents in Brighton for the weekend. They had put a movie into his DVD player— some generic romantic comedy that Ian sheepishly explained he had thought Abby would like—but conversation quickly overtook their interest in the film.

Abby was surprised by how easy it was to talk to Ian.

Sure, there was some initial first-date awkwardness, and sure, she was still sitting a good four feet away from him on the couch, but talking to Ian was almost like talking to Dani. Abby didn't feel that she had to monitor herself at all. For the past half hour she'd been telling him about the difficulties that she had with her parents back home.

"So you think they're too hard on you?" he asked.

She shrugged. "It's not that, so much. They don't exactly pressure me. I mean, they hardly have to. I always study and do well in my classes. But they treat me like I'm seven years old."

"Instead of the sophisticated sixteen-year-old that you are," Ian teased. He sat up on the couch, moving closer to her.

"Right, I forgot, because you're so much older and wiser," Abby quipped.

"And don't forget better looking," he replied.

Abby sighed, feigning exasperation.

"So if it wasn't grades, then it must have been the boys," Ian decided. "I'm guessing your mum and dad weren't too keen on you dating?"

Abby nodded.

"And what did you do about it?" he asked, a knowing lilt to his voice.

Abby flushed. "I swear, it was the *first* time in my life that I ever lied to them! I honestly didn't mean anything by it."

"But then you got attached."

"Exactly," she said. Suddenly the air in the room felt close and hot.

"What happened with him?" Ian asked softly.

Abby thought of James, briefly. His thick, curly hair, his warm eyes, the tilt of his gait as they walked down the street together. The weight of his palm against her own.

"We broke up," she said.

If Ian thought anything of this, he was sensitive enough not to say so. Instead, he patted at the space beside him on the sofa. Abby inched closer to him. The room felt warmer still and she could hear her heartbeat thudding louder in her ears.

"It must be so strange for you, then, on your own in a foreign country," he observed.

"Yes. But I'm glad for it. The opportunity, I mean."

"How'd you get your parents to go for it? If they're as strict as you say?"

Abby laughed shortly. "You wouldn't believe me if I told you. I didn't—it was their idea. Something to do with the lesser of two evils."

"Ah," he said. He put his hand on her knee and leaned closer to her, so close that his face was mere inches from her own.

"And would they go for this?" he asked, his voice bare-ly a whisper.

Abby paused. Ian's hand on her knee carried with it a sense of urgency that felt inviting, and also vaguely exciting.

She had kissed boys before James, of course, at parties and school dances—any place where boys and girls congregated socially that allowed her to elude the watchful eyes of her parents—but she'd done little else. The only person she'd ever known with *any* kind of intimacy was James. Ian, on the other hand, was foreign. Like England. And England was turning out to be a fabulous adventure, wasn't it? Abby made a decision. She locked gazes with Ian and placed her hand over his own. "No," she said, brushing her lips against his. "But they're not here right now, are they?"

"Okay, so you're telling me there was smoochage?"

Abby and Zoe were enjoying Sunday-afternoon cappuccinos at a local coffee bar. The bar was a real find for the two of them, as the norm in England was to chat over tea. They had just come from Hyde Park, where they had visited Speakers' Corner, which was, literally, a corner where anyone who wanted to basically stood up—soapbox or no—and preached about anything that came to mind. Zoe had suggested that Abby take a stand, but Abby had demurred, declaring herself "unaffiliated." Now they were sitting cozily rehashing Abby's date with Ian.

"Zoe, a lady doesn't kiss and tell."

"So that's a yes, then."

Abby reached over and swatted her friend. "It's not a no," she admitted. The tin ring of her cell phone distracted

her and she glanced at it briefly. "My mother," she said. She switched the phone off and shoved it deeper into her bag.

Zoe shook her head. "You're going to be in trouble, girl."

"I'll tell her we lost the connection. We were on the tube or something." Abby shrugged.

"Look at you!" Zoe exclaimed. "Very bold! I take it you're not going to tell her about Ian?"

Abby shook her head. "*Definitely* not. As it is, she's getting weekly progress reports from Reuben about my life, and I have to check in all the time. If there's one tiny fraction of my life that's my own, I'd like to keep it that way. Besides, she would have a conniption. They sent me over here to get away from a boy, remember?"

"Right, you told me." Zoe stirred her coffee, adding another heaping mound of sugar to the frothy concoction. "Have you heard from the ex at all lately?"

"I *think* he's finally given up," she said. "He wrote me when I first got here and I never wrote back. So maybe he gets it now? The whole thing about me needing space, that is."

"*Are* you going to write him back, ever?"

"Eventually. Probably." Abby frowned. "Can we change the subject?"

Zoe grinned. "Only if you're willing to talk about the smooch with Ian."

•　•　•

Why is this called the Whispering Gallery?" Abby asked. She lowered her voice. "Are we supposed to be whispering?"

Since their first date, Ian had appointed himself Abby's tour guide of London. His first act in his unofficial capacity was to take her through St. Paul's Cathedral, which, much to Abby's embarrassment, was located just a few blocks away from City College. He had walked her through the galleries and under the dome, where she marveled at the detailed mosaics. Now they stood inside the Whispering Gallery, the name of which had sparked Abby's curiosity.

Ian laughed. "No, you can speak as loudly as you fancy," he assured her. "But if you lean in and whisper against the wall, the sound will travel along the wall all the way to the other side."

Abby looked around the room, which had to be at least a hundred feet across. There was no way a whisper could carry that far.

"You're pulling my leg," she said, giving Ian a playful shove and a smile. "That sounds like a Londoner's version of an urban legend."

"Cheeky," Ian scolded. He grinned back at her. "Let's give it a go, shall we?"

Abby looked up at the impressive dome of the cathedral as Ian loped across the room. When he reached the wall opposite her, he signaled for her to put her head to

the wall, then leaned in and whispered something. Abby could see his lips move, but she didn't hear a thing.

She was just about to pull her head away when she suddenly heard Ian's voice say, clear as a bell, "Fancy a kiss, luv?"

Abby jumped. It was as though Ian were right next to her, whispering in her ear, even though he was still all the way across the room.

Abby whispered back, "Yes indeed." After a beat, Ian smiled broadly. He strode back across the gallery and took her hand, pulling him close to her.

Abby looked up at Ian and paused. She knew it wasn't exactly the most appropriate place for a kiss, but she just couldn't resist. She smiled mischievously and planted one right on his lips.

To: mara16@email.com
From: acapshaw1@email.com
Subject: missing in action

Yes, Mara, I know, I have been, but with good reason. The latest? Westminster Abby has a boyfriend.

We met pretty early on, soon after I got here, and we went on our first date a week ago. Now, hardly am I one to ditch my friends the minute there's a boy in the picture (as if I could—please, there've only been two boys in my life, ever), but we have seen each other nearly every day since then. And he's been acting as an unofficial tour guide of sorts for my friends and me. Though he's actually from Manchester, in Northern England, and is in his first year at "university" (imagine that I'm saying it in a veddy veddy proper accent), so I think he's kind of faking the expertise at least 20 percent of the time.

Anyway, Ian showed us St. Paul's Cathedral, and we also toured Tower Bridge and the Crown Jewels. Last week, we went to the rebuilt Globe Theatre, which, I'll admit, was slightly unexciting since I think they put it up on the site of the original sometime in 1997. One of Ian's roommates is an amateur DJ who loves trance music (points if you know what that is, and bonus points if you can let me know—and soon!), so at some point we're all going clubbing.

But the most exciting news of all? Next weekend Ian's taking me to Manchester! Yup, I'm going to meet the 'rents! He really wants to show me the city where he grew up and I think it will be cool to see more of England than just London. I read that Liverpool and Manchester together produced ten of the biggest rock stars of the century, but off the top of my head I can only come up with the Beatles, so again—if you can think of who I'm missing, just give a shout. Pretty please.

I have to admit, I'm a little nervous about the trip. This all happened so quickly. Originally Ian wanted to go for the

whole weekend, but since it's only two hours on the train we decided to do a day trip instead. I've already cleared it with Reuben, who told me that it was my responsibility to let my mom know. I'm sure he's dealt with overprotective parents before, and I think he's tired of feeling like a babysitter. I promised I would, and I did (sort of). I told her I was visiting the North for the day with a friend. Yet another in my recent spate of white lies. Is that what independence is about? I'm still not sure.

Anyway, I'm sorry to drop such big news—big to me, anyway—and run, but I'm supposed to meet Zoe in Chinatown. She had a craving for dim sum. Cross your fingers for me that I'm a hit up north! I may have to do a little shopping in anticipation; I'm feeling the need for a lucky skirt or the like.

    miss you!
    —Abby

Manchester is one of Britain's largest metropolitan conurbations. As you would expect of Britain's second city, Manchester is the throbbing urban centre of the North West boasting a number of leading business organisations, leading retailers, and entertainment venues.

"Abby, over there!"

"Huh?"

"My parents. Over there!"

"Oh!" Abby looked up to see Ian pointing at a couple just a few feet ahead, beaming wildly. She quickly shoved the guidebook she'd been reading on the train into her tote bag before having a chance to wonder what a *conurbation* was. She supposed it didn't really matter, and she could always look it up later, anyway.

Abby self-consciously smoothed her hair. She hadn't had a chance to check herself in a mirror after the ride, and she wasn't feeling her freshest. But judging from the looks on Ian's parents' faces, no one minded in the least. She could see, now, where Ian got his sparkling green eyes, because his father was grinning at her with the very same ones. And while his mother was petite and curvy, Ian's father was tall with the same broad chest that Abby adored. Both looked incredibly happy to meet her. Which helped her nerves some, but not all.

"Abby," Ian said, "these are my parents."

"Pleased to meet you," Abby said, holding out her hand to shake.

"Likewise, dear. I'm Eleanor, and this is Marcus. We're so thrilled to have you! We hadn't figured on Ian coming home over the summer, so this is a real treat." She winked. "And we never get to meet his 'friends.'" She placed special emphasis on the word *friends*, much to Abby's embarrassment.

Ian groaned and leaned in to Abby. "Are you sure you're ready for this?"

Abby wasn't sure, actually. But she was there, so it was time to get ready.

The car ride from the train station to Ian's house was short but winding as the car cut a twisted path through old, picturesque country roads. Stone walls lined the motorway and sheep grazed lazily on gray-green fields. This was the England of Brontë novels, the England that Abby had fantasized about through many an English-class lecture. She pressed her face against the window, taking in the view from the backseat.

"So Ian didn't have any problems reserving the train tickets?" Eleanor asked.

"No, of course not." Abby laughed.

"You see, Mum? She thinks I'm competent," Ian said, grinning.

"Well, then, I suppose that means you've never told her about the time when you were eleven and you completely forgot to turn in the order form for your football uniform and nearly had to play in the buff," his mother quipped.

Ian flushed. "I was saving that story until after she was hooked on me."

"Oh, well, then there's no hope, is there?" Marcus teased. "Better off just having out with it now."

"What did you do?" Abby asked, amused at the thought

of an eleven-year-old Ian streaking across a soccer field.

"The coach had an extra kit he kept in his office for sorry little boys like me," Ian explained.

"Yes, unfortunately, it was about three sizes too big," Eleanor said, shrieking with laughter. "And every time he went to kick the ball, his trousers would slip!"

Marcus roared with laughter at the memory, and Eleanor hiccuped and wiped hysterical tears from her eyes.

"Really, you both, it's not that funny," Ian said, pretending to be offended. "Scarred me for life, it did. I was going to play for Manchester United, until that afternoon. Now I can't hardly go near a football without the terrible memories of flashing my knickers in front of half of my class."

"And their parents," Marcus pointed out helpfully.

Ian leaned across the backseat to whisper to Abby. "These aren't *really* my parents." He winked. "Just some old geezers I paid off so's you'd have a chance to see more of the country. They were *supposed* to pretend that they liked me."

"Maybe you should have paid them more?" Abby suggested.

Once they arrived at the house, Eleanor showed Abby around. The house was Tudor style, small but comfortable and elegantly furnished, with a proper English garden out back. It was overgrown with thick, lush foliage and Abby yearned to crawl onto one of the benches perched among

the flowers and read. Unfortunately, though, the weather wasn't cooperating. A thin mist had settled over the countryside, casting a damp chill throughout the house. Instead of sitting in the garden, Eleanor had made a steaming pot of tea, and they'd all sat in the parlor (English for "living room," Abby discovered), sipping at it and chatting contentedly.

After they'd sat for a while, Ian suggested they go for a drive and see some of the local sights.

"Where?" Abby asked. "I have some suggestions from the guidebook, but I want you to choose so that I can see the things that are important to you."

Ian scrunched his face up in concentration, an expression of his that Abby had come to adore. "Well, we could drive to the outskirts of the city and take some nice country walks," he suggested. "It's actually not raining at the moment, though I'm sure that will change. Or we could head over to the university; it's really something to see. Very vibrant and alive, in a very different way than City College is."

"That could be interesting," Abby agreed.

"Oh, Ian, just come out and suggest it," his mother said impatiently as she sipped her tea.

"What?" Abby asked. "Does he have a favorite place that he's not telling me about."

"It's a bit embarrassing," Ian confessed.

"If you haven't noticed," Marcus interjected, "our boy's a bit of a romantic at heart. When he was little he absolutely loved going to visit the local stately homes."

"Where the royalty stay when they are in town and such," Ian said, reading Abby's quizzical look. "We have a few of them out here. They're very, ah, elaborate."

"He used to tell us he was going to be Prince William when he grew up," Eleanor said, smiling fondly at the memory. "We didn't have the heart to explain to him that it didn't quite work that way."

Abby didn't bother to suppress her laughter. "That's hysterical," she exclaimed. "Of course now we *have* to go there. I've never seen a stately home before. Is it different from a palace?"

"Well, they don't have guards out front the way that Buckingham Palace does, and the one that I love, Tatton Park, has one of the top ten gardens of the century."

The idea was instantly appealing to Abby. She loved the thought of visiting a British royal estate, and imagined herself traipsing through the garden like a character out of a period film. "Is it nearby?" she asked eagerly.

"It's in Cheshire, so we'll have to drive. But it's a short ride," Ian said. "That is, if Mum will lend me the car."

Eleanor sighed heavily, but her eyes twinkled. "Just this once, luv. Since it's a special occasion."

Tatton Park was as breathtaking as Abby had imagined. The mansion itself, Ian explained, was less impressive than some of the other stately homes he'd seen, belonging as it had to a family of "sometime local importance." But Abby

was blown away by the Georgian architecture, and secretly thought it'd be cool to be known as "sometime locally important." They toured the mansions and wondered at the eclectic assortment of collectibles to be found, such as an enormous room filled with antique keys of every size and shape, or the library, a dusty room whose floor-to-ceiling bookshelves were stocked with rare books worth, Abby knew, more than some luxury cars.

After they'd been through the open areas of the house, Ian explained to Abby that the grounds contained more than fifty acres of garden. The most notable of the formal gardens was the Japanese one, designed in 1910 by Japanese landscape artists in the West. That seemed as good a reason as any to Abby to have a look at it, and the two of them headed off on a stroll, hand in hand.

"Your parents are great," Abby offered, stepping delicately down a shrub-lined path. The weather had held out for them, but patches of the ground were still muddy from earlier rains, and she had visions of slipping embarrassingly. "It's cute how you all get along so well."

"You just like how they give me a hard time." He smiled.

"That, too," she admitted. "But it's nice that you're so comfortable with each other. I wish my parents and I had that."

"Have you tried asking them to treat you more like a grown-up?" Ian suggested.

Abby nodded glumly. "They were stunned, of course.

Reminded me that I'm 'only sixteen.' They seem to think I should be flattered that they let me stay home by myself sometimes—like it's some big show of confidence in my abilities not to burn the apartment down."

"*Apartment,*" Ian repeated in his best "Noo-Yawk" accent.

Abby shoved him playfully. "I do not sound like that. We're not *all* refugees from a bad Mafia movie. We can be quite as refined as you Brits," she finished in a clipped English accent of her own.

"Very nice," Ian said. "I can see you've been practicing."

"I hardly need the practice anymore, given how much time I spend with you. Reuben says you should be getting a cut of his salary, seeing as how you've become the de facto tour guide for my friends and me," Abby said.

"Well, if he's offering, I wouldn't say no," Ian joked.

"Seriously, though, it's so nice of you to take us all around. I know Zoe really appreciates it. She loves seeing the country through a native's eyes."

Ian stepped in front of Abby, stopping her in her tracks. She stumbled on a small pebble and he put his hands on her shoulders to steady her. Abby couldn't help but notice that even after she'd regained her footing, he didn't let go.

"What?" she asked. They had sidled up to a tall hedge and suddenly it felt like they were the only two people around for miles.

"You," he said softly. "I like you. And I hate the fact that

eventually you'll be going back to New York." He didn't say it in the funny voice this time. In fact, there was nothing funny about the expression on his face anymore.

Abby shifted uncomfortably. She liked Ian, too. She liked him a lot. But as angry as she was with James, he wasn't completely gone from her thoughts. "I'm not going back for a while," she said. "Not for at least another month." She wrapped her arms around Ian's waist and stepped closer to him.

"That's a while," he conceded. "That's a little while, at least."

"It is," Abby agreed. "And it still feels like I just got here—like it's still the beginning somehow."

She looked up at Ian, searching his face. She needn't have been confused, though; it was an open book. There was no questioning his devotion to her. For Abby, the sensation that enveloped her was pure warmth and comfort. She had fled to England, hurt, confused, and unsure of herself. And in little more than a month, she had made friends—with people unlike any she'd ever known. She'd learned to navigate a brand-new city, all on her own. And she'd met Ian, who had helped her to finally move past the pain of her experience with James. Before she'd met Ian, she hadn't thought she would ever be able to trust a boy again. Not after what happened with James. But Ian had surprised her, and then she had surprised herself. Because in two short months, Abby had done the unthinkable.

She'd gone and fallen for someone.

And she'd fallen for someone who had fallen for her right back. She might not have been ready to tell him so just yet—it was all so new and overwhelming—but she knew that the emotions would keep. That Ian would be there for her. And that when she was ready, she would be able to tell him how she felt, and that he would feel the same way.

"The beginning," Ian mused, cupping her face with his hands. "I like the sound of that."

And then he leaned forward to kiss her gently.

Chapter Eight

"So, what did you think of my fine hometown?" Ian asked.
"Do you feel that you've gotten an adequate glimpse into
my inner psyche now that you've spent quality time with
my parents and seen my childhood bedroom?"

"It's all coming together now," Abby said. "I almost sort
of wish it weren't," she added as an afterthought.

"Cheeky!" he said, reaching out to ruffle her hair. "Be
nice."

"Just kidding," Abby said hastily.

After Tatton Park, Abby and Ian had enjoyed an early
and leisurely dinner with Ian's parents. She had heard all

about the Sunday "roasts" for which England was known, and Ian's mother was kind enough to pull one together on a Saturday. The guidebooks all said they were the pinnacle of traditional English cuisine, and at this point, a very full Abby was inclined to agree. After the evening meal, she was thinking of going vegetarian for a while. Then again, she knew that she'd be starving and longing for home cooking again by tomorrow morning—just in time for another dreary City dining-hall breakfast.

Dinner was followed by pudding (another generic term that Abby was to learn actually meant "dessert" rather than something manufactured by Jell-O) and, of course, tea. Abby and Ian had prostrated themselves across the couch in the sitting room for a spell, hoping to digest a bit before they had to leave for the train station.

Now they were walking the three blocks from the train back to Finsbury Hall. The soles of her shoes were clacking loudly against the pavement. Suddenly Abby realized how truly exhausted she was. While the day had been both wonderful as well as a much-needed break from the frenetic pace of London, it had also been emotionally intense. She felt worn-out.

She stopped short in front of the entrance to the dorms. She could hear the laughter of students inside, all geared up for their Saturday night. Meanwhile, all she wanted to do was crawl under the covers with a magazine and maybe a square or two of Cadbury's.

Ian sidled up next to her on the curb. "Well, I don't know about you, but I'm knackered. Going home certainly takes a lot of energy."

"Are you sorry we went?" Abby asked, suddenly nervous and nearly forgetting that she'd been thinking the exact same thing herself.

He looked at her as if she were speaking Chinese. "Don't be ridiculous," he said, patting her shoulder reassuringly. "But please don't take it personally if I head back to mine to sleep."

She smiled. "I totally understand. I'm sort of asleep standing up, myself. You know, I can just walk myself up. You should go home. Relax. Watch bad TV."

"Which would basically include anything that Sky's airing, right?" Ian teased, referring to Abby's shock at discovering that while the British cable network did broadcast the most popular American shows, it was usually at least one season behind.

She nodded. "Exactly."

"I will do," he assured her. "After I take you upstairs and tuck you in." He grinned at her mischievously.

"Sounds perfect," she said.

She pushed the front door open and walked into the dorm. She was just about to round the corner to the elevator bank when she heard someone calling to her. "Abby! Hey—Abby!"

Abby froze. The voice was familiar. The shiver of anticipation she'd been riding on shifted to a cold fist of dread
clenched deep within her stomach. This was not indigestion. This was not motion sickness. This was recognition, a
gut recognition of something deeply, distressingly off.

Someone was here, in London, on Abby's turf. Someone
who didn't know the new and improved, independent
"Westminster Abby." Someone who didn't deserve to, either.

"Thank *God* you're back! I've been waiting all night."

Abby whirled around to see her visitor, standing before
her in the lobby with a bedraggled, forlorn expression on
his face.

"Hi, James." She sighed. "Long time no see."

It had taken Abby a split second to put two and two
together as to how and why James was suddenly standing
before her in the lobby of Finsbury Hall. The realization
landed like an anvil in a cartoon strip; he had used the
ticket she'd given him way back, when she'd first found out
she was going.

Before she learned that he had been cheating on her
for the better part of four months.

After they'd broken up, she hadn't bothered to collect
the ticket back from him. She had made it clear she didn't
want to talk to him or otherwise be in contact and she had
assumed that he would respect her wishes.

Clearly, she had assumed wrong.

Long time no see, Abby had said.

James had burst out laughing. Abby could tell from his posture that he was nervous, which was fine by her. After all, for her part, she was fairly certain that everyone in the lobby could hear the rush of blood throbbing in her own ears. She was on the verge of a complete and total break-down. *James!* She hadn't seen him since May, since the night Spencer confided in Dani that their childhood friend, little Abby, was being mistreated by her first-ever boyfriend. Spencer had agonized over the decision to betray James, but ultimately, his overprotective, brotherly loyalties won out.

Standing in the Finsbury Hall lobby, James laughed awkwardly and Abby, paralyzed, let the tote bag she had been carrying slide from her shoulder onto the ground. It hit the floor with a thud, making her start.

It wasn't until Abby turned to pick the bag up that she remembered about Ian. He'd been standing, waiting to walk Abby up to her bedroom. Now he was frozen in place, surveying James with a mixture of curiosity, dismay, and disgust. Abby couldn't believe she'd forgotten about him—even for an instant. "Ian, this is—" she began.

"James, I presume," Ian cut in. "I've heard a lot about you. Though I must admit I am a bit surprised to see you here."

"Well, I can't say I've heard anything about you," James replied.

"Right." Ian stuffed his hands into his pockets, looking lost. "You know, Abby, it looks like you've got this under control, so why don't I just head back to my flat?"

"No, but—" Abby began. *Stay,* she wanted to implore him. She knew it was unfair. She couldn't blame him for wanting to get as far away from this WB drama gone awry as possible. But she also didn't want to be left alone with James. After nearly six months of keeping all her feelings inside, she had no idea what to say, or how to go about saying it.

"I'll talk to you later," Ian said quietly, with finality. He stepped soundlessly out of the lobby.

Abby watched him go, helplessly, before turning back to a still-smirking James. What now? She wanted to go after Ian, but she couldn't just leave James standing there in the lobby. No, James was the more immediate concern. She'd have to talk to Ian later on.

Abby took James to the Nag's Head, a pub just down the street and around the corner, adjacent to the Barbican Centre. During the weekdays it was mostly patronized by bankers and other financiers on their happy hour, most of whom liked to make a pit stop before boarding the tube at Liverpool Station. Students, of course, preferred the hall bar, with its subsidized sundries, but on a Saturday night, the place was swinging with locals.

"So on a scale of one to abhorrent," James asked abruptly, breaking into Abby's thoughts, "how horrible,

exactly, am I? Honestly, Abby, I've never seen that look in your eyes before."

Abby narrowed her eyes even farther. "Well, James, to be perfectly clear, you haven't seen *any* look in my eye in about two months. Because you haven't seen *me*."

"That was at your request," he pointed out. "I wanted to talk. You were clearly not interested."

"Try *upset*. Try *angry*. It's not that I wasn't interested," she replied, "it's that nothing you could say would change the fact that you *cheated* on me. And so yes, I guess I wasn't interested. And to be honest," she finished, her voice crackling with bitter tension, "I'm not particularly interested now, either."

"Abby," James said, "come on. You said that you loved me."

"I could say the same thing to you!" she protested. "I'm not the one who was having another relationship on the side!" She turned to him with the full force of her rage, eyes blazing. "You *knew* how I felt about you, James, and you decided to completely disregard it. You *knew* how my parents felt about me dating—and particularly about dating you!"

"You said yourself your parents were overprotective," he pointed out. "You thought it was ridiculous."

"Sure, of course! But that doesn't mean that disobeying their wishes was the right thing to do! I mean, going behind their backs, *lying* to them—that's hardly a convincing argument for getting them to start trusting me to make my own decisions!"

"Well, no one put a gun to your head, Abby," James said, a touch defensive. "I was just a guy who liked you. I mean, sue me."

"You're missing the point." Abby sighed. "I liked you, too. I *loved* you," she clarified hastily. "So much that I went behind my parents' backs. And that obviously didn't mean anything to you."

"It was just one girl, Abby," James said, his voice rising. "It was a mistake. And it's not going to happen again."

Abby's eyes filled with tears. "You really don't get it," she said, looking away from him. "That almost makes it worse. If it had been more than one girl—lots of girls—I could have just told myself that they didn't mean anything. But you were having a *relationship* with someone the entire time that you were involved with me."

"It *didn't* mean anything," James insisted.

"Then why did you do it?" Abby asked, struggling to keep her voice even.

James took a sip of his beer before answering the question. He looked at Abby, considering. "This is going to sound twisted," he began, "but I got scared."

Abby rolled her eyes. "That is so typical."

"I'm sorry!" he said. "I know it's lame, but it's the truth.

I've never felt about anyone the way I felt about you—*feel* about you—and I freaked!"

Abby cocked her head in disbelief. "So you cheated on me because you cared so much?"

"Yeah," he said. "I did."

"Why did you come here?" Abby demanded suddenly, sitting up straight in her seat and looking directly into his eyes.

"You wouldn't take any of my calls. You wouldn't reply to my e-mails. I had to talk to you."

"All right, so I told you I didn't want to see you anymore, and I deliberately avoided any contact with you. So what the hell was so important that you had to come all the way here to see me?"

"Abby, I love you," James said, his voice hoarse and thick with desperation.

"Please," she said. "Forget it."

"Do you think I came here for *fun*?" he asked. "I'm being straight with you. I knew you weren't exactly going to welcome me with open arms. I'm here because I love you. I've never loved anyone else. It's the truth, Abby. I'm telling you the truth."

"For the first time in months," Abby said. "Remind me why I should even listen to what you have to say."

"Jeez, Abby, how about, 'because you care'? You know, you're different here."

"You mean because I'm not a pushover? Because I

actually see you for who you are and refuse to fall for your lines? Yeah, I guess I am different." Abby folded her arms across her chest defiantly. "But do you want to know something? I like who I am these days. I was terrified to come to London, but after you cheated on me, there wasn't much reason to sit at home and feel sorry for myself. And since I got here, I've made friends, I've seen amazing sights, I've been on my own for the first time ever," Abby said.

"That guy you saw? In the dorms? Yeah, that's my *boyfriend*, James. His name is Ian. He's from Manchester, and we just spent the day together up north with his *parents*. Can you imagine that? A guy who likes me, wants to be with me, and isn't distracted by other girls? Apparently the new me isn't too bad." She paused, her breath coming in short, sharp gasps.

"I'm telling you that I loved the *old* you just fine," James said, his voice softer now. He reached out and laid his fingers across her forearm. "I don't blame you for being angry. I violated your trust. I get that. But believe me when I say it was the biggest mistake I ever made. And I've regretted it ever since."

Abby felt woozy. Ever since she had broken up with James, she had fantasized about him saying those very words to her. True, she hadn't ever given him the opportunity, but the image had persisted just the same. She had replayed this scene in her head dozens of times, and still, the images from her mind's eye couldn't begin to compare

to the satisfaction—and the emotional swell—that the reality brought. She had to admit, she was tempted. James had been her first love. And he was here. Asking—no, *begging*—for her back.

The old Abby would have just melted, said yes without even thinking about what she really wanted, Abby thought.

But that was then, and this was now.

Now there were other issues to consider. There was the question of trust. No matter what James said, she would always wonder if he was genuinely committed to her. Especially if he was in the U.S. while she was in England for another month. A month was a long time to spend apart from someone. Especially someone with wandering eyes.

Then there was the whole idea of the "new" Abby. This Abby was independent, adventurous, and knew how to make decisions for herself. This Abby could stand on her own two feet. She had gotten by just fine without James for the last three months. She didn't need to rush back to him now, just because he said he was ready.

And, of course, there was Ian. She was falling in love with Ian, pure and simple. She knew Ian felt the same way, and she knew that unlike James, he was someone she could rely upon. She didn't want to hurt him, and more than that, she didn't think she wanted to leave him.

But compelling as these reasons were, they didn't completely erase the wave of affection and familiarity that

James's presence brought over her. She slid farther back against the edge of the couch. Everything about James— the spring of his hair, the gleam in his eyes, the curve of his jaw—it was all calling out to her. She had to restrain herself from reaching across the couch and pulling him into her arms. In the time that they'd been apart, she thought she had built up a tolerance to him; an anti-James immunity. But no. He was like her Achilles' heel. The romantic equivalent of Kryptonite.

She shook her head, willing the sentimentality to melt off, to give way to reason. She had too many thoughts racing through her mind, and each was directing her differently. It was giving her a headache.

"I don't know, James," she said finally. "I think it's too late."

"But you're not sure?" he asked hopefully.

She shook her head. "I'm not. I'm not sure of anything." She looked at him. "Where will you stay while you're here?"

"I can crash in a hostel."

Abby glanced at her watch. Nine P.M. The closest youth hostel didn't close its front desk until midnight. "Fine," she said. "You can meet me at Finsbury in the morning."

Fortunately, the light was on in Zoe's room when Abby stopped by. She could hear the strains of subdued eighties

New Age angst music wafting from under the door. She rapped on the door and Zoe answered it, wearing cotton pajama pants, a tank top, and an expression of complete unsurprise.

Zoe stepped backward from the door and swept her arm out in front of her, indicating for Abby to enter. "Please," she said, "I need all the dirt on Hurricane James." She stepped aside to let Abby pass. "You're lucky I called it an early night."

Abby sighed. "Did you see Ian?"

"Just a bit ago, at the hall bar, hunched over a beer, looking heartbroken," Zoe confirmed. She padded across the room, reaching for a tin that sat atop her desk and holding it out to Abby. "Twizzlers," she said. "With love, from Mom. Eat. Sit. Tell." She settled herself school-style on her bed.

Abby collapsed on the opposite side of the bed, leaning against the wall and facing Zoe. All of the rooms in Finsbury were set up the same way, so Zoe's was identical to Abby's, with an identical view of St. Paul's. It hadn't been all that long ago that Ian had given her a private tour of the cathedral, Abby realized, but enough had happened since then that it felt like forever.

"What did Ian say, exactly?" Abby asked, not completely sure that she wanted to hear the answer. She waved away the Twizzlers. Her stomach was knotted with anxiety; the last thing she needed was a sugar rush.

Zoe swallowed. "Not too much. Just that James had

shown up, you seemed freaked, and he didn't want to cramp your style. Mostly he was just moping. I had to extrapolate a lot."

"But he seemed upset?"

"Yes. The sad, self-pitying stuff of bad Lifetime movies," Zoe said matter-of-factly. "I think he went home, though. So where's James now?"

"Well, we went to the Nag's Head and talked, but the whole thing was really stressful," Abby said. "I don't know what to think."

"He wants you back," Zoe guessed.

Abby nodded. "He's really sorry. He says it's the biggest mistake he ever made."

"You're not buying it?"

"I *wish* I weren't buying it," Abby said. "The smart, reasonable Abby knows not to. I mean, cheating? Not a good sign."

"And the emotional, heartbroken Abby?" Zoe prompted.

"I have to admit, it felt good to hear him tell me he was wrong," Abby said. "I guess I had sort of wanted to hear that all along. And I did love him. Maybe I still do. But things are more complicated now."

"Because of Ian." It was a statement of fact, not a question.

"Yeah. Manchester was amazing. His family is so warm and friendly—you can see where he gets it from—and things are going really well for us. I mean, it would probably

be pretty dumb to throw that away for someone who doesn't seem to know how to commit."

"Sure," Zoe said. "That's the rational side of things. Ian good, James bad. But it's not always so easy to separate emotions from reality, right? If it were, you would have just shown James the door."

Abby shrugged guiltily. "Yeah."

"So what did you tell him?"

"Nothing, yet," Abby said. "Just that I was confused and that I really didn't know. He's staying at a hostel tonight. I told him I would meet him tomorrow." She sighed. "I guess I'm just a little torn. Ian's probably going to be mad that I didn't just kick James back to the States. And I can hardly blame him."

"Well, yeah, probably. But this is your life and you have to do what's best for you. Which may involve seeing this thing out with James. Otherwise, you may always wonder. And how will that be helpful for you in the long run, with or without Ian?"

"You're right," Abby said slowly. She reached up and pulled her hair into a sloppy ponytail, suddenly realizing how very bone-weary she felt. "You're totally right."

"When's the return flight on James's ticket?" Zoe asked meaningfully.

Abby made a face. "A week from now. But he could probably change it if he wanted to."

"Of *course* he can change it." Zoe ripped the cellophane off another Twizzler and scarfed it down. "Sorry," she said, waving the red vine apologetically. "Dinner was awful tonight. I hope you stuffed your face in Manchester."

"We did," Abby assured her. "I don't think I'm going to be able to eat for a week."

"That works," Zoe said. "Anyway, like I was saying. I'm sure he could change his ticket. It would probably cost him money, but so what? It's his fault for coming over here without even checking with you to be sure that you'd be willing to talk to him. The question is, what do *you* want him to do?"

"I don't know," Abby said. "I really don't know. I still have to call my mom, you know. Tomorrow. Sunday. Our appointed check-in time. I was already planning on lying to her about Ian. Or, at least, hiding the truth. She'd flip if she knew James were here. So that's two lies now. When I came here, I wanted to have a little freedom. *Not* completely lose any shred of credibility I may have had."

"I hardly think you're a psychopathic liar," Zoe interjected. "But I see your point. Get some rest. You'll feel better in the morning."

"Okay." Abby nodded. But deep down, she wasn't so sure.

Zoe had said that Ian would probably be back home by this hour, but Abby took a chance and found him in the

hall bar, sitting by himself. It was one-thirty and people were just starting to head home.

"Hey," Abby said, edging up to Ian tentatively. "I thought you were going home to crash."

Ian tilted his head up to meet Abby's gaze. "Wasn't quite ready to toss it in after all," he said. Abby wasn't sure whether or not his words carried a double meaning.

"Did you eat?" she asked.

When he didn't reply, she reached out to smooth his hair back from his forehead. He flinched, though, as her hand drew near. "What are you doing, Abby?" he asked. "Is he staying with you?" He sounded sad.

"I don't know," she said, her eyes watery with confusion, exhaustion, and distress. "It's not my fault he's here, you know."

"Fine, I'll give you that," he said, sitting up straighter in his seat. "But you have the final say on how long his visit lasts, don't you?"

Abby looked down, unable to meet his eyes. In one motion, Ian rose swiftly from the bar, slapped a bill down, and nodded in the direction of the bartender. "Well," he said, "give me a call once you've sorted things out."

Then he was gone.

Chapter Nine

On Sunday morning, Abby found James just outside the dorm, puffing contentedly on a cigarette.

"Hey," he said, seeing her emerge from the building. "Perfect timing." He dropped his cigarette butt to the ground and smashed it with his heel. "I'm starving."

She shuddered at the sight of the butt on the ground. "That is such a gross habit," she said.

He ignored her pointedly, and she started down the street in the direction of the financial district, James in tow. She figured they could have something to eat at the coffee shop that she and Zoe liked to frequent. "I've been

thinking," James said as they rounded a corner past a row of banks, "we should go away this coming weekend. To Dublin. It's close by, and easy to get to."

Abby stopped dead in her tracks and stared at him. "James, please. I offered to let you stay, but really. I'm not sure I'm ready to go away with you. I mean, I just spent yesterday in Manchester with Ian," she reminded him.

He shot her a look of utter disbelief. "Abby, I accept that you've met someone here, but don't tell me you're over us, just like that," he insisted. "I wanted to come here and visit with you, but I think it would be good for us to go away together for a few days, to be alone on neutral territory. Think it over, at least?" he asked, his voice dropping an octave. "I hear the Guinness brewery tour is really fun."

Abby wasn't totally convinced, but she had to admit that he made a decent point about being on neutral turf. But still . . . "We'd have to go Thursday," she pointed out. "Because we need to be back Saturday for your flight. That doesn't give me so much time to think."

"If we go to Dublin, we can take a flight out of Heathrow on Thursday afternoon after your classes and get there in a few hours. I read that you can totally tour the city in a day or two. We'll hit the sights Thursday evening and Friday. I can probably even change my flight so I can go back to New York direct from Ireland on Saturday, and then you can go back to London."

Abby was shocked. He had clearly done his homework

with regard to the trip. "I have class on Friday," she said. "Just one. A psych section."

"Well, I would never tell you to miss class," James said, "but I really do think the trip could be great." When Abby was silent, he continued, imploring yet again, "Please just think about it. Promise me you'll do that."

Abby sighed heavily. She seemed to be doing that a lot—sighing—ever since James had arrived. "Fine," she said. "I'll think about it, but that's it. No promises. I'll let you know Tuesday in time to book the tickets. There's a student travel agency on campus that can hook us up. But no whining if my answer is no," she finished sternly.

He held up his hand. "Scout's honor," he said.

And in that moment, Abby could have sworn that for all the world, he sounded sincere.

"'One thousand seven hundred tons of steel have been used in the construction of the London Eye. That's more than the weight of two hundred and fifty double-decker buses.'"

"James, will you *please* put the guidebook away? You're being such an American it's embarrassing!" Abby whispered loudly, giving the term *American* roughly the same respect one would accord a "baby-eating sewer demon." She didn't bother to mention that she was usually the one with her nose buried in *Fodor's* while Zoe ignored her. Apparently she and James did have something in

common, after all. How could she possibly have forgotten?

But for today, at least, she could play the worldly ex-pat, living abroad on her own time and her own terms. James, certainly, seemed fooled by her little role-play. After breakfast, they had walked through the East End and the financial district, Abby pointing out her favorite neighborhood haunts. They'd taken a brief peek at the public galleries at the Barbican, too, before grabbing lunch at a chip shop. James was unconvinced of the merits of vinegar over ketchup as a condiment—that was, until he bit into his first thick, chewy chip. "Excellent," he had reluctantly admitted. "Different from McDonald's, but excellent."

Later, they took the tube to the London Eye, an immense, rotating observatory sponsored by British Airways. As Abby had been forewarned, the "queue" was obscene. But James, who'd been quoting enthusiastically from his guidebook since they started their hike, was completely undaunted. He threw an arm across Abby's shoulder amiably. "Over seventeen hundred people in five countries were involved in building the Eye."

"And they're all standing on line to ride it now," Abby said, warily eyeballing the distance to the front of the line. "James, we're going to be here forever."

"Abby, the Eye is one of the foremost attractions in the world," James said, adopting what could best be described as a college-professor tone. "And you're going to ride it!"

Abby shuddered. "Have I mentioned I'm terrified of heights?"

"Since we've actually been to the Empire State Building together, I'm going to point out that 'terrified' is a *slight* exaggeration," James said. "But don't worry, babe, I won't let you fall out." He squeezed her shoulders tightly.

"Wait, they don't have doors that latch?" Abby asked, suddenly panicked.

James burst out laughing. "They have doors, Abby," he assured her. "You are not going to fall out." He waved the guidebook at her teasingly. "The doors are actually really cool. They were designed by some super mechanical engineers. You want to know how they were manufactured?"

Abby glared at him. "You have no idea how much I don't. If we're really going up there, then ignorance is bliss."

James chuckled again, then leaned over to kiss her on the cheek. Abby bristled. If this day, this easy banter, the peaceful sightseeing, was an attempt to get under her skin, it was working. But that didn't mean she was ready for all of the physical contact James was so carelessly flinging her way.

They entertained themselves by quizzing each other from the guidebook while they waited for their turn on the Eye (in truth, Abby suspected that James was far more entertained than she was by this game). One hour and fifty

impromptu *Jeopardy*-style bonus rounds later and Abby was nervously stepping aboard their own *Jetsons* capsule, willing it not to wobble back and forth. James ambled in after her, beaming eagerly. After the pod was filled to capacity, the attendant slid the glass door shut, and with a final totter, they slowly climbed upward. Abby squeezed her eyes shut.

"Abby, if you keep your eyes closed, there's no way you're going to see 'Windsor in the west,'" James said.

"I'm okay with that," Abby replied, welding her fingers over her eyes for good measure. "Really. I've seen Windsor already."

James pulled at her fingers but she slapped him away. "Since when are you such a 'fraidy cat?" he teased.

"Since you somehow talked me into voluntarily paying money to be shuttled one hundred and thirty-five meters aboveground in a glass pod. I mean, really. This is not the great glass elevator. I can see no good reason why we, as sane people, deliberately signed on for this."

"*You* signed on for it because of my brilliant powers of persuasion."

"Oh, right," Abby said.

She carefully peeled open one eye so as to better shoot daggers at him. But what she saw when she did caused her to freeze, breathless. "Oh."

"Yeah, that's what you'd be missing if you kept hiding

behind those pretty little hands," James said, laughing at her expression.

Abby gazed out the window, agape. If she had thought the view from the river's edge was pretty, then this was spectacular. From here she could see the whole of the city, even—as James had so thoughtfully read to her—Windsor in the west. As the pod slowly rose higher into the air, the peak of Big Ben blurred to a tiny, obscure dot on the horizon. She could see the Millennium Bridge, linking the Tate Modern to the city of London, and she could see, closer still, the stunning avant-garde architectural feat that was the Bridge of Aspiration, a multiangled glass sculpture that connected the Royal Ballet to the Royal Opera House.

"There's Westminster Abbey!" she cried with delight.

James leaned forward, pressing his forehead against the glass. "I think we're too high up, babe. There's no way you can tell Westminster Abbey apart from St. Paul's at this altitude."

She shoved him lightly. "It takes thirty minutes to fully rotate on this thing. We've been riding for less than ten. We're not *that* high up yet. And anyway, you underestimate me. I can spot Westminster Abbey from any direction, any distance. We have, like, a connection."

"You and the building?" James asked, smiling at the thought. "You're psychically linked?"

"It's my namesake," Abby said. She frowned. "Or, I

guess, vice versa." The pod shifted slightly in the wind and her stomach lurched. She reached out and grabbed at James's arm for support. He hugged her to him.

"I've got you," he said.

At that moment, Abby didn't know exactly what came over her. Maybe she was light-headed from the altitude, or maybe there wasn't enough oxygen circulating in the glass car. It could have been adrenaline, a by-product of her acute fear of heights. Or it could have just been the prox-imity of James's body to her own, the scent of his musky deodorant mixing with the light fragrance of her shampoo. All she knew was that all at once, she felt dizzy. And not a bad kind of dizzy. This dizzy was something she could hold on to.

James stopped as though he suddenly realized the way that Abby was looking at him. "What?" he asked quietly. After a beat, he tuned in. He reached out and smoothed Abby's hair from her forehead.

She leaned over and kissed him. It was quick, but soft and full. She drew back again hesitantly.

"Oh," he said. "That."

Without saying anything, Abby took James's face in her hands and gently tilted it toward the windows so that they were once again taking in the view. She clasped his hand in her own. She wasn't sure quite exactly what was hap-pening between them, but she knew, somehow, that for the immediate future, it was right. Whatever "it" was.

The other thing Abby knew then and there, beyond any last droplet of residual doubt, was that next weekend, she and James were going to Dublin.

"So you're *sure* you want to be dealt into this hand, now?" Zoe asked, taunting. She shuffled the deck of cards like a professional casino dealer. Abby made a mental note to ask her friend where she'd learned this later on. And maybe to get a tutorial for herself.

"Oh, I'm sure, sweetie," James replied.

James, Abby, Zoe, Simon, Chrissy, Melanie, and Fred were gathered in the hall bar enjoying a round of cards. Everyone except Abby was apparently rather well versed in poker and so she had volunteered to "keep score," which ultimately deteriorated into needling whichever player was losing most drastically.

"He's on a roll, luv," Simon said.

Abby was relieved to see James fitting right in with her friends. Not that she was surprised—his charisma was one of the very first things that had drawn her to him—but Zoe, in particular, was aware of their history, and Abby had been slightly worried that her friend's protective instincts were going to emerge in a not-so-gracious way. It turned out that all of her fretting had been in vain. Zoe had clearly decided that if Abby was okay with James, then so was she.

They played, talked, and laughed for a good couple of hours, no one in any particular rush to get to bed. Abby

was snickering over an unfortunate jukebox selection when the door to the hall bar swung open. Instantly, the wind was knocked out of her. The boy who strode in was Rob, Ian's roommate. Ian, whom Abby realized she really hadn't thought about all day. At least not since the electric moment she and James had shared on the London Eye. She briefly allowed herself the fleeting hope that Rob was alone.

That hope lasted exactly three seconds, at which point Ian loped through the door on his friend's heels. He looked freshly showered and poised for a night on the town, but his tight, anxious expression belied the gelled party-boy effect. He scanned the room. As his gaze swept across Abby and her cohorts, his eyes glazed over and his face froze into a wall of stone.

Ian tapped Rob on the arm and indicated that he was going for a drink. Ian spanned the distance from the door to the bar in three quick strides, walking right past Abby's table without saying anything. Abby flushed.

Her subtle shift of composure did not escape James's attention. "Isn't that your. . . ?" he asked. He didn't seem to know how to finish the question, though.

Abby nodded mutely.

"Maybe you should go talk to him?" he suggested.

Abby flashed him a grateful look for being so under-standing, pushed her chair out, and quickly crossed to the bar.

Ian remained glued in place at the bar in a practiced

nonexpression. "So I see James is still here," he said with resignation.

Abby blushed. "Yes, but I'm not sure how long he's staying. I couldn't exactly *force* him to leave."

Ian sighed, but said nothing.

"That's it? Don't you want to talk?" Abby implored.

"What would you have me say?" he asked.

"I don't know," she said. "But you *must* have something on your mind or you wouldn't have come down here, right?" Or so she hoped.

"What, I was supposed to hide out from the hall bar just because you and James *might* be here? Not likely, Abby."

"No, okay, I get that," she said, backtracking. "You're right. And maybe I should have gone somewhere else."

Ian turned to her. "No, you should stay. It'll be fun. You, me, and your ex-boyfriend. One big happy family."

"That's not true," Abby said, her throat catching. "You know that's not true. He came without asking me, Ian. I don't know what you expected me to do."

Ian sighed again. "Nothing, Abby. I don't expect you to do anything. You need to figure this out on your own time, I know."

And with that, he left his drink, turned, and stalked off, leaving Abby alone, in his wake.

"So he's furious?"

Zoe and Abby were back in Abby's room, drinking tea

and rehashing the finer points of Abby's confrontation with Ian.

"Not exactly, but he's definitely not happy. Can you blame him?" Abby sighed. "You know, before this past school year, I'd never had a boyfriend in my life. Now I'm totally torn between two guys."

"Yeah, I wish I had your problems," Zoe teased.

Abby glared at her. "I'm serious. When James and I were on the Eye, it was so romantic, I almost completely forgot about Ian. But then, of course, seeing him . . . I'm supposed to just choose? I can't! But of course, I can't expect to just string both of them along indefinitely, either."

Zoe shook her head. "Alas, no. But it sure could be fun." She smiled. "But everything is all set for your trip?"

Abby nodded. "Yeah, James made all of the travel arrangements. He insisted on paying for the plane tickets because he's been working this summer. He gets a student discount, anyway. And I spoke to Reuben. He's cool with it all. I mean, he has my cell and I have his number. We're covered."

"Another 'don't ask, don't tell' situation?"

"If my mother asks—which I'm assuming she will—he'll tell her I went to Dublin for the weekend with a friend. But I'm going to call her preemptively and let her know, too. It's not his job to cover my butt."

"Is your guilt in overdrive?"

Abby looked at her friend. "You have no idea."

Chapter Ten

"I swear, I think their legs are going to catch fire or something. I mean, that just can't be natural, can it?"

Abby laughed and followed James's gaze to where a team of Irish step dancers were stomping on the wooden floor, pounding out a beat in time with the fiddle band that accompanied them.

They'd arrived in Dublin on Thursday night, as James had suggested, and found their way to their hostel. It wasn't fancy, but it was clean—or, at least, semiclean—and it was cheap. They'd dropped their backpacks off and made their way into town to check out the Irish pub culture, stopping

off at haunts supposedly once-frequented by the likes of Bono, James Joyce, and even Sinéad O'Connor.

They'd spent Friday morning exploring the city on foot. Fortunately, it wasn't very big, so they were able to cover a lot of ground in a relatively short amount of time. They saw the Christ Church Cathedral, which was the oldest building in Dublin. Afterward, they toured the campus of Trinity College. Just beyond Trinity lay a small shopping center, which Abby forced James to explore just long enough to discover that really, there wasn't much difference between a mall in Ireland and a mall in the U.S.

After walking for most of the afternoon, they were both exhausted, but their hostel had a lockout between the hours of eleven and six. James had wanted to visit the Guinness brewery, anyway. They had taken a tour of the factory, where Abby learned way more about the distilling of beer than she would ever need to know. There had even been a little film-strip, which James had watched raptly.

The whole experience was totally fun, but, of course, Ian was always in the back of Abby's mind. She hadn't had a chance to talk to him again before she left for Dublin, and she was worried that he was going to find out about her trip from someone else. That would upset him even more, understandably. All afternoon, Abby tried to find a time to call Ian just to check in and try to smooth things over, but James was always at her side. At the brewery she had finally ducked into the "loo" for a last-ditch effort, but her

call went straight through to Ian's voice mail. She didn't
bother to leave a message.

Instead she decided to make the best of her time in
Dublin with James. The question of a reconciliation with
James had, thankfully, taken a back burner for the time
being. The best way to figure things out was to let herself
just "be" with James, which was what she was doing.

They ate an early dinner—more fish and chips—and
consulted the trusty guidebook yet again for information
about nightlife. James was determined to catch some
authentic Irish step dancing. Abby pointed out that most of
the step dancing showcased in Dublin would be deliberately geared toward tourists, and for that reason perhaps
not legitimately "authentic," but he wasn't daunted. Hence
their seat, front row and center, at this small-scale *Lord of
the Dance*.

"It looks a little bit like tap dancing," Abby said, strain-
ing to be heard over the music.

"Huh?" James asked.

She leaned into him, her lips hovering just next to his
ear. She was acutely aware of their proximity. "I said, it
looks like tap dancing," she repeated. "Some of the steps."

"That's right." James grinned. "I forgot you used to tap.
I bet you'd kick ass at this, then."

Abby couldn't figure out where the wicked glint in his
eyes had come from. All at once, though, she realized that
the step dancers had broken out of formation and were

each step-hopping down the aisles of the pub-turned-dance-hall to rouse willing victims from their seat to join in. James half stood in his seat, motioning frantically toward Abby, volunteering her.

Abby's eyes widened in panic. "Absolutely not!" she hissed. Okay, it was true; she'd become a bit more outgoing since she had left home. But there was *no way* she was going to get up there and embarrass herself in front of the whole pub. It had been years since she'd taken tap dance, and besides, she hadn't been that good at it, even in her heyday. They always stuck her in the back during recitals.

It didn't matter, though. A smiling woman in full costume was clomping straight toward her like a crazed windup doll, hands on hips and stomping away at top step-hop speed. Her creamy complexion was flushed with exertion and her bright green eyes sparkled. Her twin brunette braids bounced with every gesture. The whole thing actually might have been somewhat inviting if only it hadn't been for the pesky mortification factor.

Abby shot James a pleading look but he only laughed and tangoed toward a petticoated dancer of his own. Apparently James had no issues with public humiliation.

Abby knew, really, that her only option was to go along and join in. She didn't want to be the wet-blanket wallflower, after all. Reluctantly, she held out her arms so that the dancer could place them back on her hips properly.

Once she had nailed the posture issue, she fell in line behind the dancer and studiously surveyed her feet's movements. The steps were tricky, and Abby knew she wouldn't be winning any dance trophies anytime soon, but she could keep up well enough.

She fleetingly hoped she didn't look dumb. But when she looked up, she noticed that no one else in the pub was at all concerned with her or whether or not she looked foolish. They were all up, flooding the aisles to dance, not at all worried about how they looked. It finally dawned on Abby that she probably would have looked more foolish if she'd sulked in the corner rather than trying out the dancing. And at least this way, much to her surprise, she was actually having fun.

As she stomped out her own beat on the floor, she glanced up again and caught James's eye. He was jigging in place energetically and looking right at her. She smiled at him and waved. And then stumbled directly into an awkwardly placed chair, tripping flat on her face. *Now* she looked stupid, all right.

She slowly pulled herself up and glanced back at James. Yup, he was laughing at her. At first she was flustered. Then the humor of the situation dawned on her. Before she knew it, Abby was laughing herself. James tangoed toward her, clicking imaginary castanets in time with the music. Abby doubled over. He swooped down and pulled her back to her feet, swiftly moving into a waltz.

Before Abby could protest, James had dipped her backward. He pressed himself against her folded figure and kissed her. As a general rule, Abby was opposed to public displays of affection. She hated to think of other restaurant patrons oogling them. But then she remembered that she wasn't supposed to be caring what other people thought of her. Abby closed her eyes and kissed James right back.

"Abby!"

No, thank you. Sleeping.

"Abby!" The disembodied voice was more insistent now. Sensing urgency, Abby sat straight up in bed.

"You *have* to get up. *Now.*"

She recognized the voice, at least. That was James's voice. She sat up at full attention. The hostel was empty, bunk beds stripped of linens.

James sat at the edge of his bunk looking more than a little worse for the wear. His hair was rumpled and unbrushed, and his clothing was wrinkled as though he had slept in it. Which, come to think of it, maybe he had. Abby looked down at her own body and was unsurprised to find herself wearing her jeans.

"What happened?" she asked, her voice thick with sleep.

"Um, well, I think we both passed out last night," James said. "We were pretty beat."

"Well, at least it makes getting ready easier," she chirped. "We won't need to change."

"About that." James exhaled. "We were so tired, we, ah, forgot to set the alarm."

Abby peered at him. "Forgot?"

"Or maybe we set it wrong. Either way, babe, we overslept. In case you haven't noticed, we're alone in here. Lockout starts in fifteen minutes."

Abby's eyes flew open, the mental cobwebs disappearing in a poof of anxiety-driven smoke. "You're kidding me."

"I wish I were, Abbs. But, we're running a little behind. More than a little."

Like a shot, Abby was up from the bed and on her feet. "Well, you can't miss your plane," she said, her voice taking on the clipped tone of a manic drill sergeant. "You handle checkout, I'll pack for both of us. And maybe you can pick us up something to eat."

James chuckled at her no-nonsense approach to getting it all together. "It's a plan. And may I say I like your take-charge attitude?"

Abby glared at him. "Then why aren't you moving?"

James took one look at her expression and decided she wasn't kidding. He darted from the room in search of food.

Shaking her head, Abby gathered their clothing together. She balled it up into two separate piles and started shoving them into their bags.

Her cell phone hit the bed and bounced backward,

faceup. She glanced at the screen. Two missed calls. A feeling of dread washed over her. She checked the caller ID and her fears were instantly confirmed. *Ian.* He had called her twice since she tried him from the bathroom at the brewery. Did he know that she had gone away with James? Did he know she had tried to get in touch? Either way, he was probably as angry as ever.

"This really wasn't the way that I wanted our good-bye to go," James said.

"Well, it's not ideal," Abby admitted, "but what can you do?"

James opened his mouth to respond to her but was jostled by a hurried passenger making a beeline for the escalator.

They stood in the airport terminal. As he had explained, James had rearranged his ticket so that he could go directly home to New York from Dublin. Abby wanted to see him off at his gate; then she would take another flight back to England on her own. It had made sense when they planned it, but Abby suddenly wished she had just a few more hours with him. It didn't help that they had been rushed out of bed after oversleeping and had spent the morning in a frantic rush. The airport was bright and noisy, thrumming with energy and people in a hurry. James was right; it wasn't the place for a long, romantic good-bye.

But for now, it was the only place that they had.

"I'm not being flippant," Abby apologized. "I had a great time with you this week. I'm glad you came to visit. It didn't feel right, hating you. I like this better, where we can at least care about each other."

"At least?" James asked, looking hurt. "Abby, I came here to England specifically so that you would know how I felt. I never once stopped caring about you. And . . . well, I promised you it would never happen again, didn't I?"

Abby thought about pointing out that he had a strange way of showing it. But she decided that was beside the point by now. "I know," she said simply, reaching out to smooth her hair out of her face and then stuffing her hands back into her pockets. "I do know that."

"But you just aren't sure that you feel the same way anymore?" James asked.

Abby shook her head. "James, I have no idea what I'm feeling right now. A week ago, I would have said that I never wanted to see you again. But like I told you, I'm really glad that you decided to come. It means a lot to me that you wanted to show me how you feel. I had a great time with you, and I'd sort of forgotten that we used to have great times. And of course, I still have feelings for you."

"So, what's the problem, then?" James asked, reaching out to touch her cheek lightly.

"The problem is that you violated my trust, James, and you really hurt me. And I think it takes more than just a week to rebuild after a violation like that. Not to mention,

there are other people's feelings at stake here now, too," she said, not wanting to mention Ian by name.

"You really care for him, huh," James said.

Abby nodded again, blinking back tears. "I do." She paused. "But it's more than that. I care about both of you, but this isn't about making a choice. It's not a one-or-the-other thing. It's more that I think I need time. For myself. You know, to figure things out."

"I'm not going to wait around forever, you know," James said.

"And I'm not going to be bullied, or pressured into making a decision that I'm not ready to make," Abby said, matching his determined tone.

"You're right," James relented. "I'm probably being unfair. But I want you to know how serious I am about you. About us."

"I get it," Abby promised him. "I really do."

James smiled. "You're different these days, Abby," he said. "Very different."

She cocked her head inquisitively. "Bad different or good different?"

He took a deep breath. "I think it's good, yes. More self-confident. Self-assured. Like, you know who you are."

"It's true," Abby agreed. "I think it was being on my own that did it. But I have to say, it feels really good."

"It suits you," James said. He wrapped her in a bear hug.

Abby allowed herself to breathe in James's scent. She grasped tightly at his arms with her own. She'd miss him, she knew.

But she also knew that she was ready for him to leave.

She pulled away from him, looking him in the eye. "That's your flight that's boarding. You should go."

"Yeah," he said. "We busted our butts to get here on time, after all."

She smiled and reached up on her tiptoes to kiss him good-bye. Their lips touched briefly, and then they were separate beings again, James making a big, awkward show of gathering his luggage and straightening his clothing. "Well, I'll see you," he said gruffly.

"Definitely," Abby replied. "I'll be home soon."

"You don't want it to fly by, though," he said.

"That's true." She nodded. She knew that it would, but she also knew that she wouldn't take even a moment of it for granted. She was well beyond that point by now. If she could have reset the time barrier to move in slo-mo, she would have. That was how badly she wanted to draw out her London adventure.

"Keep in touch, James," she said, offering a small, hopeful smile. "I'll miss you."

He half nodded, half wagged his chin in her general direction. She couldn't help but notice that his eyes were red-rimmed and watery. She'd spent enough time after their breakup looking that way to recognize the symptoms

of heartbreak. And while she felt for him, it didn't change the way she felt about their situation.

She stayed long enough to watch James get in line to board his flight. The line moved forward at the pace of a tortoise moving through cement, but soon enough, he had reached the front. He turned once, waved, and then he was gone.

Chapter Eleven

Finsbury Hall was uncharacteristically quiet by the time Abby returned home on Saturday night. She was okay with that, though; the bumpy flight home had left her feeling queasy. A half liter of ginger ale had become her new best friend. She dragged her exhausted body up to her bedroom and changed into her most comfortable track pants and T-shirt.

She wasn't ready to go to bed just yet, but she really wasn't up for socializing. She hesitantly began to unpack her bag and came upon her cell phone, which was tucked into the side pocket of the backpack. She realized that she

had never checked her voice mail after she saw that Ian had called, so she dialed the number and entered her password.

One new message. "Hey, Abby." Ian's voice echoed over the line, then paused for a beat. "I, uh, heard that you are in Dublin for the weekend." Abby's stomach dropped. "I hope you and James are having a lovely time." There was definitely anger in his voice now. "At any rate," he continued, "I saw that I had missed a call from you—and I'm not sure why you're calling if you're with him, but—"Ian's voice broke off and Abby could hear him take a deep breath. "If you want to talk, I'll listen."

Abby wasn't sure what to think or feel. On impulse, she decided to try to reach Ian, but chickened out when she got his voice mail again. It was probably for the best, though, she reasoned. She just didn't know what to say to Ian. After a weekend with James, she needed some down-time to clear her head.

She took the elevator straight down to the basement and headed to the computer lab, which thankfully was empty. She quickly logged on.

From: Danishoe@email.com
To: acapshaw1@email.com
Subject: what's up?

Hello, world traveler!

I'm dying to know what's new and exciting over in the European Union! Of course I'm *really* dying to know how your week was with *James*! I can't believe that he surprised you like that, and I'm amazed that you decided to let him stay. That doesn't sound like something you would do. In fact, it sort of sounds like something that *I* would do. I guess England *has* had that kind of positive, risk-taking effect on you. And Dublin—I'm thinking you wouldn't have gone if you two weren't getting along. So please, without further delay—I must have the details. I'm hoping you're okay about all of this.

I miss you tons but I hope you're having way too much fun to miss me back. Write soon and let me know what's the what.

I hope you've been practicing your British accent. I rented *Trainspotting* this weekend to feel closer to you and watched more than an hour of it before I realized they were in Scotland. Oops.

☺,

me

Abby glanced at her watch. It was eleven-thirty. That meant it was six-thirty in New York. Dinner in the Capshaw household usually started at seven. If she called now there was a decent chance she could talk to her parents. She figured she could get a jump start on Sunday check-in day.

She went back to her bedroom and fished her international cell phone out of her purse. She tied her hair back and settled in on her bed, dialing the main number for her parents' house.

"Hey, Mom!" Abby said brightly, when her mother picked up the line. "What's going on?"

"Oh, you know, the usual craziness. I just got back from the organic-food market. Do you think Daddy will want turkey meat loaf for dinner?"

"I think Daddy is lucky that you even manage to find time to cook with all of the work you have," Abby said, knowing it was the response her mother wanted to hear.

"You're sweet. And you're certainly up late! Never mind, then. I spoke to Reuben this weekend; he tells me you were in Dublin?"

Abby swallowed. "Yeah, my friends and I went." She hated hearing the lie trip off of her tongue. "I tried to reach you before I left."

"Yes, well, travel is wonderful, dear, but I do hope you've been making time for studying. When Reuben told me about all of your little excursions, I took the liberty of having a look at your academic calendar online. You have midterms next week, don't you? I trust you're prepared?"

"Midterms? Yes. Prepared. Of course," Abby stammered, realizing that, in fact, she had *completely* forgotten about exams. *Uh-oh.* She'd have to find Zoe and spend some time cramming before midterms started on Thursday. She'd never left studying until the last minute before. Was this also part of the new and improved Abby Capshaw? "Can't wait."

"Fabulous, dear. Listen, thanks for checking in, but I have to run or things won't be ready when your father comes back from yoga. But according to the Web site, your grades should be e-mailed to you a week after the tests. So you can just forward those along to us. Okay?"

"Perfect," Abby said, gritting her teeth. "Love you. Bye." She hung up the phone and flopped over onto her stomach in despair.

Perfect, indeed.

Zoe's door swung open to reveal a very grumpy-looking green-haired girl, dressed for bed in an oversize Sex Pistols concert T-shirt. "This had better be good." She squinted at Abby. "I know you expected more from a party person like myself, but I've been sleeping for an hour. In your absence this weekend, I was forced to hang out with more boring people, and as a result, I am grouchy. This is not my finest hour."

"Actually, I know exactly what you're talking about," Abby said. "I'm in a horrible mood."

"Are you, now?" Zoe asked, raising an eyebrow. "Well, I'm still not psyched that you woke me up." Nevertheless,

she stepped aside and let Abby into her room, padding back toward her bed and burying herself back underneath her covers. "I'm assuming you have a good reason for being here?"

Abby nodded. "Midterms."

"Huh?" Zoe stared at her. "You were thinking I might have some here, just on hand or whatever?"

"Midterms," Abby repeated. "As in, exams. They start on Thursday. Have you studied?"

"Um, maybe not in the strictest sense, no," Zoe admitted. "But we've both at least been to the library this semester, and from what I understand, that gives us a solid shot at a C. Which should be enough. I know you're an overachiever and all, but this semester is pass-fail for you, right?"

Abby sighed. "Yes, but my parents want me to e-mail them my grades."

"So you e-mail them that you passed."

"I told you, they're a little bit psycho-overprotective. They're going to want to see the letter grades, regardless," Abby said. "I shouldn't be so surprised. This is totally typical for them."

Zoe hugged her knees into her chest, looking thoughtful. "Well, does that mean that they expect you to get As?"

"Probably," Abby said, chewing at a nail intently. "But I'll settle for Bs and take the heat."

"Fab," Zoe said, nodding slowly. "Then Bs it is." She leaned over and flicked off the switch to her bedside lamp, engulfing the room in darkness. "We'll just get right on that first thing tomorrow, 'kay?"

From: acapshaw1@email.com

To: capshawclan@email.com

Subject: the results are in

Hi Mom and Dad!

Well, midterm grades are in! For the record, it was As in Brit Cinema and Shakespeare, and Bs in Social Policy and Psych. I think I must have spent at least seventy-two hours straight in the library but at least it paid off!

Now, if I know you both, you're going to be disappointed that it wasn't straight As. But this semester is about more than just grades.

The fact is, I'm taking these classes pass-fail, so I'm totally satisfied with the Bs. Especially because I honestly do think that being here has taught me lots about myself that has nothing to do with classrooms. I'm learning about who I am and I'm learning to be on my own. And for me, those are invaluable lessons.

There's one other thing that I'm learning, too. And that's the value of honesty.

So I'll be straight with you.

When you first sent me here, I was angry that you were so involved in what I thought were my decisions, my life. And since I've come to London, I've totally resented the

way that you both keep tabs on me all of the time. I would be happy to fill you in on everything I'm doing here—it's all so exciting!—but I don't like you always checking up on me with Reuben. So I kept some things from you—things that I knew would bother you.

I know you think I went to Manchester with a friend, and I did. But it wasn't any old friend, it was a boyfriend. Now I know you think I'm too young to be dating, but he's great. Honest, outgoing, and reliable. Of course it almost doesn't matter, because we're not together right now. And the reason we're not together is because of another thing I didn't tell you.

James came to visit me.

I didn't want him to—we broke up before I left for England, but I had given him a plane ticket ages ago and he decided to use it. He stayed in a hostel, and we went to Dublin together (separate beds, of course). He thought we should have some time together, and eventually, I decided he was right. Not to mention, it was fabulous to have a chance to see another city. I promise you that James and I did not get back together or anything. But we did have some unresolved issues to work out.

I don't blame you if you're furious. But can you at least try to understand where I'm coming from?

I'm so thankful that you both agreed to send me here, and I truly hope that you both can see things my way this time.

Lots of love,

Abby

From: capshawclan@email.com

To: acapshaw1@email.com

Subject: Re: the results are in

Well, Abby, I'm not sure where to begin. I'm stunned to learn that you've been, if not lying to us, at the very least misleading us all this time. Obviously, when your father and I heard that you were going to Manchester and Dublin with friends, we never once assumed that you were going with boys. Had we known, we certainly would not have approved.

This is not what we expected when we gave you this opportunity to study abroad. If we genuinely believed that you were merely exercising some newfound independence, that would be one thing. But of course, this smacks of something far less wholesome.

And to know that the lying is merely the tip of the iceberg! To hear that you've let your academics slip! We were afraid that you were taking too much advantage of your time abroad, but we never suspected it would extend so far as to get in the way of your studies. We can't pretend to be impressed by any grade of B or below.

That said, however, you are correct in reminding us that these grades do not transfer to your transcript and thus

they don't "count" insofar as college admission is concerned. As for the issue of the degree to which they "count" for your father and me—particularly in light of other information you've finally passed along—we'll have to give the matter further thought.

—Mom

"So she just signed it 'Mom'?" Zoe asked, wide-eyed.

Abby nodded glumly. "Oh, yeah. And don't forget the part where she's 'giving the matter further thought.'"

"What the heck does that even mean, anyway?" Zoe demanded. "I mean, are they going to decide that you can't stay in England?" Her eyelids flew up her forehead again. "Wait—they're not going to decide *that*, are they?"

"I seriously doubt it, but I suppose you never—uf!" Abby tripped over an unturned stone and wobbled for a moment before steadying herself.

She and Zoe were enjoying a bright summer afternoon hiking in the Cotswolds, an enchanting network of picturesque towns and villages set against rolling countryside. Judging from the number of hikers they encountered on their trek, they weren't the only ones who had decided to take advantage of the good weather.

Abby straightened herself out and stepped more daintily over a protruding root. "This is too much physical exertion," she complained. "As a general rule I like to avoid exercise."

"Hey," Zoe said. "We've been holed up studying for days. We needed fresh air. It's good for us."

"I'm tired of things that are 'good for me,'" Abby complained. "My whole life has been 'good for me.'"

"Well, wasn't that what the whole thing with James was about?" Zoe pointed out.

"In the beginning, maybe," Abby said. "I definitely wanted to try something new, which I guess meant dating. But the thing is that I really loved him, so eventually it wasn't about the shock value anymore. I would have stayed with him no matter what. But I certainly wasn't *trying* to do the right thing. Or the wrong thing. Or whatever."

She paused. "I wasn't *trying* to annoy my parents. That was just sort of a by-product. Anyway," she decided, "I don't *think* they'll make me come home early. I mean, what would be the point? I won't be able to get into my regular classes at school this late in the semester anyway. So from a 'productivity' point of view, this makes more sense."

"Yes, and productivity is key," Zoe said, sounding skeptical. "Oooh, look!" She pointed toward a spot on the horizon. "It's a little stone wall. How quaint. And sheep! Let's go see the sheep!" Before Abby could reply, Zoe had grabbed her hand. "We must skip. Let's skip!" She hopped off by way of demonstration.

"I'm not much of a skipper, Zoe!" Abby shouted. It was useless, though. Zoe was on a sheep-driven mission.

When Abby reached the wall, Zoe was already leaning

against it, beating out a rhythm with two twigs she'd found on the ground. "The sheep aren't big into drumming," she observed, sounding disappointed. She tossed her makeshift drumsticks to the ground and waved her fists at the sheep in mock despair. "Oh, it's no use." She hoisted herself up onto the wall. "Stupid sheep."

"This looks a lot like Manchester," Abby observed. "Lots of stone walls and sheep. Well, not actually Manchester itself, 'cause that was a big city. But on the way there. We saw tons of sheep and rolling hills. I think that's basically the gist of England. You've got your cities, and you've got your rolling hills. With the sheep."

"Could be," Zoe said. She tilted herself forward, her expression growing a bit more serious. "And speaking of Manchester, *what* is the deal with you and Ian, girl? You two have gone well out of your respective ways to avoid contact for the past week. I think I saw him dive behind the jukebox when you walked into the hall bar last night."

"Yeah, we haven't spoken since before I left for Dublin. I told you, he called while I was there, but I didn't answer. And when I went to call him back, he totally blew me off. What am I supposed to do, stalk him?"

"Right, bad idea," Zoe agreed. "But now that you're not going to be with James, maybe it's worth another shot? I mean, you dig the guy, right? At the very least, it would be nice not to have to hide under a table every time he walks into the hall bar, right?"

"I guess." Abby sighed. "I mean, yes. Of course. I would love to make up with him. But after that whole week with James I was really drained. And he's so angry and hurt, and I just don't even know what to begin to say. I have no idea if we should even be together, anymore. But yeah, I want to make it right. Definitely. Whatever that means."

She didn't know, but she would have to find out. And soon.

Chapter Twelve

"Capshaw residence."

"Hi, Mom."

Abby and Zoe had come home from the Cotswolds late Saturday evening. Zoe had decided to go to a pub with Simon, Fred, Chrissy, and Melanie, but Abby was exhausted. She was also feeling guilty about how unresolved things still were with her mother. Once the gang had gone off for the night, she called her parents from her cell.

"Hello, darling, I tried you on your cell earlier but you weren't around," Abby's mother said, cutting through the line as clearly as if she were in the next room. "What time is it in England, anyway? Oh, dear," she said, as if she'd only just consulted her watch. "It's very late. What are you doing awake at this hour?"

Abby quickly scanned her brain for a plausible excuse. "It's Saturday night, Mom."

"Well, technically, darling, it's Sunday, but what's the point in arguing. But. Now. That's not actually the reason I wanted to talk to you."

Abby's stomach clenched. This was it. Her mother was going to tell her that she had to come home. The lies about the boys and the Bs on her transcript were it. She had violated her parole; her wings were being clipped. She took a deep breath. "Yes?" she asked, without daring to exhale.

"I spoke to Reuben again after your last e-mail, dear. I wanted to get his take on the whole situation."

"And?"

"I can't tell you how much he raved on about you and your 'inner poise.' He thinks you're incredibly bright and well presented."

"Well, maybe he's right," Abby said, bristling.

"Yes, well, that's what I got to thinking, dear. That if he had gone out of his way to talk you up—and if he trusted you to go traveling on your own—then he was probably telling the truth. Unless you had somehow bribed him, which I assume you didn't."

"Um, no," Abby said, offended.

To Abby's surprise, she heard tinkling laughter across the phone lines. "I was joking, Abby," her mother said. "Of course you didn't bribe him. Anyway, the point here is that I think it's possible—now I'm only saying *possible*, not definite—that your father and I have been too hard on you. After all, as you say, the Bs aren't going to affect your transcripts, and it does seem as though you're really making the most of your time abroad."

"What are you saying, Mom?" Abby asked, a flicker of hope washing over her.

"I'm saying that I worried that you were too caught up in James, but I see now that if you were interested in dating other boys, and turned James away, then you aren't caught up at all. You're just a young woman tackling all of the choices that come along with being on your own for the first time. And you have our blessing to live your life the way that you see fit while you're over there. It certainly sounds as though you know what you're doing."

Abby did a silent shimmy across her bedroom, pumping her fist in the air. She wasn't going home! She wasn't even in trouble! Heck, it sounded like they were actually starting to trust her!

"Abby? Are you still there?"

"Yes, of course." Abby stopped dancing.

"I said, there's one condition."

"What?" Abby asked, suspicious.

"We need to know that you're not going to lie to us again. And that you're going to get straight As on your finals."

Abby paused for a moment, considering. She'd gotten two As and two Bs after three days of solid studying and a handful of visits to the library. Could she exert a tad more effort and pull off four As—even though it wasn't, in the strictest sense, *necessary?*

Yeah, she could. If it meant that her parents would respect her and give her more free rein, she absolutely could.

"Not a problem, Mom," she chirped, bouncing up and down on her toes. "As it is. And I swear—I'll never lie to you again." Now that her parents were trying to be more understanding, she didn't even feel that she had to.

"Wonderful, Abby," her mother gushed. "I knew we could count on you."

They said their good-byes and hung up the phone, leaving Abby to disco-dance across her bedroom in earnest. Her parents *knew* they could count on her. It was an amazing feeling.

But more amazing than that was a blinding realization: Abby's parents weren't the only ones who had, just recently, learned to count on Abby. Over the past three months, Abby had learned to count on herself.

• • •

"Is this what you were thinking?"

Abby craned her neck to see where Zoe was pointing. "No. Uh-uh. Too purple. I wanted more lavender."

"Right."

It was a week after Abby's conversation with her mother, and Abby and Zoe had decided to do something slightly crazy to celebrate Abby's newfound independence. Both girls realized that finals would be on them before they even knew it, and they wanted to make the most of their remaining time in England.

Zoe stood on her tiptoes and reached her fingertips toward a bottle of hair dye on the highest shelf in the booth. It came crashing down on her furiously, bringing about half a dozen other brightly colored bottles with it. Zoe assumed standard disaster crouch, shielding her head with her arms, as the bottles clattered to the ground noisily. She reached down and plucked one off the pavement, brandishing it triumphantly. "Like this?" she asked, beaming brightly.

Abby nodded. "Totally."

The owner of the booth rushed over to assess the damage. He knelt down and began to gather up the fallout. He pretended to glare at Zoe. "You're lucky I fancy you, luv," he said.

"Alistair, I'm one of your best customers, and you know it." Zoe smirked.

"You're terrible," Abby said.

She and Zoe had returned to Camden Market. They came here fairly regularly now on weekends, as it was the best location for Zoe to refine her punk-rock goddess wardrobe at minimum cost. She had a never-ending appetite for silver jewelry, cheap eyeliner, and fishnets. But today they were here for Abby. Abby was going to do something dramatic.

She was going to dye her hair.

"Now, do you want to get the bleach?" Zoe asked. "Because with brown hair—even light brown hair, like yours—you're going to have to strip it down with peroxide if you want the lavender to show in streaks like mine."

"Um, no," Abby said, after a moment's consideration. "I mean, I'm rebelling, but I'm not running out to front-line in my own band, you know. I think just the allover wash will do. Just light brown hair with a purplish hue. Does that work?"

Zoe nodded. "Definitely. And you know, I actually think it's perfect for you. I mean, it suits your personality. It's totally cool and a little bit edgy, but you know . . . temporary. Like your normal, awesome self—but with bite."

Like a scoop of vanilla —but with sprinkles, Abby mentally amended, returning to the metaphor that had come to her on her initial plane ride over. She thought back to that night, and how far she had come. That Abby had been terrified of new experiences, while this one sought them out. Abby smiled to herself.

"I'll take this one." She handed the bottle to Alistair. "I don't need a bag."

Abby was fishing her wallet out from her bag when she caught sight of Ian, wandering down the aisle. He wasn't really looking where he was going, and he was headed straight for them. Abby panicked. She had never been able to come up with the right thing to say to him after her trip to Dublin with James. She contemplated diving behind the cash register now. But no. There wasn't enough time for that, and besides, that was ridiculous. Her summer session was almost over and she couldn't bear the thought of leaving on bad terms with him. She stepped out of the aisle and directly into Ian's path.

"Hey, stranger," she said softly.

Ian nearly jumped twelve feet in the air. "Abby!" he exclaimed. "You nearly gave me a heart attack." But her stealth method seemed to have the desired effect; he hadn't really had time to get his armor up. "What are you doing here?" he asked.

She gestured to the register. "Zoe and I are"—she looked around, and then realized that Zoe must have gracefully fled the scene when she saw Ian coming in order to give them some privacy—"...were buying some... hair dye," she finished, slightly embarrassed. "Is that lame?"

"What, for Zoe to dye her hair again? Not like we haven't seen that before," he said.

"No, for *me*," Abby said. Was it so difficult to believe that *she* was the one doing something slightly adventurous?

Ian's eyes popped out of his head. "No *way!*" he cried. "That's brilliant!"

Abby's face lit up with a smile. "So you don't think it's lame?" she asked.

"Not at all," he replied. "But won't your mum and dad kill you?"

"Actually, we had a little heart-to-heart," Abby explained, "and they're sort of giving me a little more freedom to do what I want these days."

"That's fantastic," Ian said, his voice warm and sincere. He locked eyes with her. "And what, exactly, is it that you want to do?"

Abby gazed back at him, lulled by the sparkle in his green eyes and the grin playing on his lips. Was he asking what she thought he was asking? Was he beginning to forgive her? Maybe the weeks of not talking had hurt him as much as they had hurt her. Maybe he missed her.

As much as Abby missed Ian and was desperate to be on good terms again, she wasn't sure that she wanted things to go back to the way they had been. There was suddenly something appealing about being on her own. Did she still have feelings for Ian? Of course. She might even still love him. But that didn't mean that she had to rush into any decisions. Her gut was telling her that she needed time to think things through, to clear her mind

before leaping back into any serious relationships. Jumping back into his arms—even just for the little time she had left in London—could be a mistake. The last few months had been really intense. Abby owed it to herself to listen to her gut. It had served her pretty well until now.

She reached out and stroked Ian's cheek. "I'm not sure," she answered honestly. "I think I just need some time on my own."

He nodded slowly. "I can understand that," he said. "Although I do hope that there's room for me in your life somewhere."

"Of course!" Abby said. "I've always wanted that."

He looked at her, shifting his weight back and forth as though he wanted to say something more. Abby bit her lip nervously. "What about James?"

"He went back," Abby said. "I don't know what's going to happen, but we're definitely not back together."

Ian nodded slowly, but he remained silent.

"That's five quid even, luv," Alistair said, cutting in and abruptly ending the moment.

"Let me get that for you," Ian said, digging into his back pocket for his wallet.

"No, it's all right," Abby said, waving him away. "I can take care of myself." She stopped, thinking about those words. They were true. She *could* take care of herself. In England, and anywhere else.

• • •

The nightclub 333 was the hottest underground spot in Shoreditch, the trendiest neighborhood in the city. It was crowded, hot, and throbbing with energy. In her fishnets and miniskirt (courtesy of Zoe's closet), Abby found she fit right in. She'd dyed her hair that afternoon and was happily shaking her lavender locks to the beat. She hadn't ever been clubbing in New York—the closest she'd ever come were some divey live-music venues with sticky seats and sawdust-covered floors—but somehow, this scene was exactly what she had expected. She felt like a character in a movie; the makeover character who is turned into a princess and steps out on the town. Sure, in Zoe's costume she was more punk than pop, but it suited the venue. She'd never really been into trance, trip-hop, or drum-and-bass, but it didn't seem to matter. Once they hit the dance floor, she somehow found the rhythm.

Zoe, Simon, Chrissy, Melanie, and Fred had all come along to hear Ian's flatmate Rob spin, and the six of them were clustered in a circle on the floor. As Abby pulsated in sync with her friends, it dawned on her that this was the second time since she had come to England that she'd busted a move on a dance floor with no regard for public humiliation. And more than that, she hadn't been humiliated one bit. She was just another cool girl out with her friends, having a good time. In London.

She was so relieved that her parents had decided to ease up while she was here. She was going to study for

finals and hold up her end of the bargain. And Ian had promised to take them all to the London Dungeon, an offshoot of Madame Tussaud's that was kind of like a lurid house of horrors. She couldn't wait.

She was thrilled that she and Ian had run into each other at Camden Market that afternoon. It was just too weird back when things were awkward between them. They didn't have the same easy chemistry tonight that they'd had when they first met, but at least they were communicating.

Abby caught Ian's eye from across the circle that their group had formed. Seeing her looking at him, he smiled and winked. It was a look that held potential. Maybe he wasn't going to be the love of her life—especially since she was going home so soon—but you never knew. Whatever happened between them, Ian was a part of the most exciting time Abby had known. Everything had changed for her in London. And now the door for her and Ian was open. But it was more than that; for Abby, now, *all* the doors were open. And she was ready for whatever would come her way.

Acknowledgments

Muchas gracias to Eileen, Kristin, Suzanne, Angelle, and Alex, who were fabulous with guidance, understanding with deadlines, and all-around supercool in general. As always, thanks to all the Ostows for endless support. And, of course, a special shout-out to Nancy C. for the initial recommendation.

Turn the page for a special preview of another

novel:

Getting the Boot

Chapter One

Turbulence jolted Kelly Brandt out of a deep sleep as the captain announced their initial descent into Rome's Fiumicino Airport. Almost there! She looked at the view out the airplane window, expecting a fairy-tale scene below her. Instead, the neat squares of fields looked surprisingly like the Illinois farmland they had passed over on their takeoff from O'Hare.

Kelly could almost feel the Italian sunshine hitting her face. Rome was going to be awesome—delicious food, tons of culture, and shopping, shopping, shopping! She pictured handsome gondoliers rowing down moonlit canals

past chic Romans wearing cutting-edge European fashions. And there was absolutely no such thing as a bad slice of pizza. Who could live there and not end up worldly, sophisticated, and glamorous? She would return home in three months' time, a vision in flame-red lipstick and couture clothes, throwing around endearments like *cara* and *bella* without sounding like a pretentious ass.

Kelly yawned loudly and stretched her arms over her head, wondering just how long she had slept. Judging from the thick novel in her friend Sheela's lap—now halfway read—it had been quite a while. Kelly had sorely needed the rest.

The night before, her best friends, Starr and Tyffani, had thrown her a going-away party. Starr Santoro was legendary for throwing the best parties; she always attracted the hottest crowd, found the best DJs, and made kids from all over the area beg for invites. Going to a Starr party was like going to an exclusive club: If you didn't have the right look or know the right people, you couldn't get through the door. And the party she threw for Kelly's last night home had topped them all.

Normally, Sheela would never have made the invite list, and she wouldn't have cared a bit. But Kelly had insisted that Starr include her, and had begged Sheela to come along. Sheela would, after all, be Kelly's only tie to home once they got to Italy; it was key that the girls get along this summer.

Kelly had known Sheela Ramaswamy forever. Their dads had roomed together in college, and their families still got together every so often on weekends. Even though their crowds didn't mix much in school, the girls had a history that kept them together.

Sheela and Kelly had been inseparable in elementary school, but things changed in junior high. Kelly got braces, made it onto the dance team, and landed a plum role in the school play. All of a sudden she was surrounded by a tight new circle of friends, and had more and more excuses for spending less and less time with Sheela.

By the time they started high school, Sheela was every parent's dream—and every party girl's nightmare. She was responsible and mature, got fantastic grades, and stayed out of trouble. Instead of enjoying being sixteen and single with a spanking-new driver's license, Sheela was wasting the best years of her life on moldy books and the math team. If Kelly could convince her to loosen up and have some fun, maybe there was hope that they'd have a blast together in Italy.

When the two girls walked into the party, Starr and Tyff hugged Kelly as if it had been months, not hours, since they'd seen her.

"Our guest—guests—of honor have arrived!" Starr announced, ushering them in the door. "So Kel, are you ready for *bella* Roma?"

"The question is, is Roma ready for us?" Kelly laughed.

"Love your hair, Sheela," Tyff said, smiling at her.

Sheela's hand flew up to her head self-consciously. "Thanks. Kelly did it for me. And my makeup."

"Well, no wonder it looks fabulous," Starr said over her shoulder as she and Tyff ran off to greet some new arrivals.

"Since when do your buddies even know I exist, much less shower me with compliments?" Sheela whispered to Kelly.

"Since I told them that you have a pierced nipple and your boyfriend's name tattooed on your butt, and that that's why you're so shy about taking your clothes off in gym."

Sheela burst out laughing at the utter ridiculousness of this scenario. "He must be quite a guy if I'm branding his name onto my ass. Is he cute at least?"

"Beautiful. He's a Portuguese bad boy with long black hair." She gave Sheela's dark locks a flip. "And a Harley. Too bad you're gonna ditch him for a Roman hottie on a Vespa."

The way Kelly said it, it had almost seemed possible.

They made their way to the bar, where Kelly, ignoring Sheela's anxious expression, poured them each a glass of punch. Kelly's father was a corporate attorney, and he had developed a technique for making sure his daughter behaved herself at parties. Before going out, she had to sign a contract banning drugs and drinking. It was an effective approach, mostly, but Kelly had become expert at tweaking the rules here and there.

"This is spiked," Sheela said. "Didn't you promise your parents you wouldn't drink tonight?"

"Relax," Kelly answered. "I have a system. Take a few sips, then hold the glass all night. That way, nobody bugs you." Kelly waved at someone on the other side of the room. "Come on. There's someone I want you to meet."

"Freddy, Sheela. Sheela, Freddy." Kelly put a death grip on Sheela's arm so she wouldn't run away and whispered in her ear. "One gorgeous Portuguese biker boy, with my compliments." She smiled into her friend's scarlet face.

Kelly watched as Sheela cast a furtive glance at Freddy. He smiled and reached out to shake her hand. "According to Kelly, we've been dating for years. Why don't you tell me about yourself?"

Kelly let the two of them talk while she perched on the arm of a nearby couch and flirted with a few football players from school. One of them held up a lit joint. "Kel, you want a hit?"

Kelly wrinkled her nose. "Nope, not my thing. Actually, all the smoke in here is making my allergies go crazy. What I *need* to do is dance." She grabbed a partner off the couch and waved to Sheela. "Have fun, you crazy kids." She spun on her stilettos and took off.

Kelly sighed happily at the memory. The party had been

a total success. Even though Sheela had left early to finish packing, it was obvious that she had enjoyed herself. Kelly hadn't seen her laugh so much since they were little. And she'd never seen her dance before, much less with a guy. Kelly's biggest gamble, enlisting Freddy, a pal from work, to play Sheela's boyfriend, had worked like a charm.

It was an absolutely perfect send-off until the very end of the evening, when Tyff had burst into tears.

"Summer won't be the same without you. Who will I go to the beach with? The parties are totally gonna suck." She snuffled pathetically. "I'll miss you."

"Yeah, and who will *I* go shopping with?" Starr demanded. "I mean, Tyff's okay with shoes, but she can't accessorize to save her life."

Kelly put her arm around Tyff. "C'mon, guys. It's only three months. You'll be back in bags and belts in no time."

"It's not just three months," Tyffani whined. "You'll come back totally changed, and you won't want to have anything to do with us senior year. And then we'll go off to college and this will all be over."

A wave of nostalgia washed over Kelly as she gazed out the plane window; she wished all of her friends could have come to Italy with her. She had no regrets about saying good-bye to life in the dull suburbs, but she would sorely miss her crew. Exploring Rome had to be a thousand times more fun than hanging out in Chicago, but doing it alone was no good. She was thankful Sheela would be there with her, even if the girl's social skills needed a major boost.

Sheela had reverted to her bookworm ways the instant she'd left Starr's house. In fact, if she hadn't been turning a page every now and then, Kelly would have checked her pulse. It was a shame because Sheela could be lots of fun, on the rare occasions she let her guard down. She had a dry kind of wit that cracked Kelly up and a simple, direct style that was a nice break from some of the posers at school. Kelly hoped that at some point this summer, she could convince her old friend to enjoy herself a little.

Kelly actually considered it her duty to kick up their friendship a notch. After all, if it hadn't been for Sheela, Kelly would never have found out about the S.A.S.S. program, or the Programma Internazionale di Roma. S.A.S.S. was a study-abroad program for American girls that placed them in schools all around the world, and the Programma was Sheela's school of choice. Its director, Dr. Timothy Wainwright, had been Mr. Ramaswamy's adviser in grad school. Dr. Wainwright had sent Mr. R a copy of the brochure with Sheela in mind, but the moment Kelly had spied Sheela reading it in the high-school cafeteria, she had been intrigued. Even now, months later, she still couldn't stop looking through the brochure. Kelly pulled it out of her carry-on bag and flipped through it for the umpteenth time.

The cover featured a panoramic view of some ancient ruins with the sun setting majestically behind them.

Smaller photo insets showed happy-looking teenagers strolling down quaint, cobblestone streets, eating gelato, hiking in the countryside, and engaged in animated discussion in a classroom. Inside, a headline announced, EARN SCHOOL CREDITS WHILE IMMERSING YOURSELF IN THE HISTORY, LANGUAGE, AND CULTURE OF ITALY.

"You know, in a couple of hours we'll actually be there," Sheela said. "I think you can ditch the brochure already."

"I can't help it," Kelly said. "I'm just so freaking excited. What do you think the dorms are gonna be like? I'm picturing something straight out of MTV *Cribs*!"

Sheela snorted. "Except they don't have homework on *Cribs*. Seriously, Kelly, it's a school, not a spa. You're actually going to have to do some work, you know."

Kelly groaned. "Don't remind me. My parents certainly haven't let me forget." She flashed her most brilliant smile. "Luckily, I have a genius at my disposal."

"Are you saying the Ramaswamy SAT prep course wasn't enough for you?" Sheela picked up her book again. "High-quality wisdom like mine is going to cost you from now on."

Kelly laughed. "I'll keep that in mind." More seriously, she added, "I already totally owe you, Sheela."

It hadn't been easy convincing her parents—or the S.A.S.S. coordinator, or Dr. Wainwright, for that matter—that she could cut it in such a rigorous academic program, but Kelly had waged a long, hard campaign. Initially, she was wait-listed as a S.A.S.S. candidate. But then she'd been inspired to try a backdoor approach and had asked Sheela's dad for Dr. Wainwright's e-mail address. And it had worked. She brought her grades up, cut way back on socializing, and, with Sheela's help, got a far better score on her SATs than anyone would have expected. And she made sure that Dr. W was aware of each of her accomplishments. She had earned her acceptance fair and square, and now she was going to enjoy every minute of her summer abroad.

Sheela smiled slyly. "You can buy me a *stracciatella* gelato for paybacks."

Kelly blinked. "What the hell is that?"

"It's vanilla gelato with chocolate chips."

"You got it."

The plane took another gentle dip downward. Kelly pulled her purse up onto her lap and felt around inside. Mirror, brush, lip gloss, blush, mascara.

Sheela looked at her quizzically. "What are you getting all dolled up for? It's six o'clock in the morning in Rome."

Kelly smiled and shrugged. "I want to make a good impression on Italy, that's all."

"On Italian men, more like."

"Yeah, well, in celebrity mags, paparazzi are always snapping shots of stars as they get off planes. It's important to always look your best—you never know who you might bump into." She reached over to smooth Sheela's seat back–induced hair frizz and got her hand smacked.

"If Orlando Bloom happens to be loitering around the airport at the crack of dawn, I'll be out of luck. Otherwise, lay off."

Kelly looked out the window as the plane descended for landing. The weather was thick and overcast, and the plane had to circle before finally bumping onto the runway. As soon as the seat-belt sign went off, Kelly jumped up so fast she nearly blasted a hole in the overhead compartment. The girls hoisted their carry-on bags and followed the crowd to the baggage carousels.

Sheela consulted a stack of well-thumbed papers. "I guess most of the other kids are coming in on early-morning flights, too. They're sending two buses, one at eight, one at nine-thirty." She checked her watch: 6:45 A.M., Rome time. "Looks like we're in the right terminal to meet the first bus."

Kelly was barely listening. Instead, she was scanning the crowd gathered around the luggage carousels. It was easy enough to spot the Americans, but she couldn't figure out whether the others were real Italians or not. Many wore jeans and T-shirts. A group of seedy-looking taxi drivers circled around, waving signs and pinching cigarettes between tobacco-stained fingers as they searched for fares.

It took the girls quite a while to collect their suitcases and go through customs. Kelly was at a total loss when it came to understanding the customs officials, and Sheela had to do all the talking. After what seemed like forever, they collapsed onto a bench outside to wait for the bus.

"Now I know why they call this flight the red-eye," Kelly said, yawning.

"I know. I feel like we've been traveling for days." Sheela glanced at Kelly. "Hey, where's the locket your mom gave you?"

Kelly gasped, her hand flying up to her neck. She pulled the chain out from underneath her shirt. "Oh, thank God." She elbowed Sheela. "You scared the crap out of me. My parents would kill me if I lost this."

"Sorry. Can I see it again?"

Kelly proudly held out the locket. Her parents had given it to her as a going-away present when they dropped her off at the airport. It was an antique that had belonged to her mom's mother. Kelly carefully opened the shiny gold lid, running her fingers over the swirling script initials etched on its surface. The inside held an old photo of her grandmother and a new shot of her parents.

"Wow, your grandmother looked just like you when she was young," Sheela said.

"Yeah, and my mother says I'm as full of piss and vinegar as she was," Kelly said, laughing. "I still can't believe Mom gave this to me. She's worn it ever since Grandma died last year. But my granddad bought it for my grandmother when they were on their honeymoon in Rome, so I guess my mother thought it was a sign or something. She says it will be like my grandmother is watching over me

when I wear it. When she was alive, Grandma never took it off. And neither will I."

Sheela glanced down at her watch and stood up. "It's almost eight. The bus should be here soon."

Kelly carefully tucked the locket back under her shirt, grabbed her suitcases, and followed Sheela outside. The sun was burning off the last bits of fog, and the air was getting downright steamy.

A little blue bus with a sign in the window reading PRO-GRAMMA INTERNAZIONALE DI ROMA slowed to a stop a short distance past them. Kelly and Sheela rushed down the sidewalk as fast as their bags would allow. A small cluster of teens was already lining up to board.

There was a punk/Goth girl with spiky jet-black hair and thick, smudgy eyeliner, an outdoorsy-looking guy with a huge hiker's frame pack strapped to his back, and two girls whom Starr would have described as "granolas." As they got closer, Sheela's face froze into a petrified grin.

"God, I hate being sociable," she muttered.

Kelly reached out and squeezed Sheela's arm. "Relax. They're just people. Nobody's going to bite your head off." She smiled. "With your brains and my personality, we can't go wrong. Promise me you'll try to enjoy yourself."

Sheela gave her a grateful nod and took a few deep breaths. "Okay, let's do it."